Queen of the Court

Michele Martin Bossley

James Lorimer & Company Ltd., Publishers
Toronto, 2000

James Lorimer & Company Ltd. acknowledges the support of the Ontario Arts Council. We acknowledge the support of the Government of Canada through the Book Publishing Industry Development Program (BPIDP) for our publishing activities. We acknowledge the support of the Canada Council for the Arts for our publishing program.

Cover illustration: Sharif Tarabay

Canadian Cataloguing in Publication Data

Bossley, Michele Martin
    Queen of the court

(Sports stories)
ISBN 1-55028-703-6 (bound)   ISBN 1-55028-702-8 (pbk.)

I. Title. II. Series: Sports stories (Toronto, Ont.).

PS8553.O7394Q43 2000   jC813'.54   C00-930193-3
PZ7.B67Qu 2000

James Lorimer & Company Ltd.,   Distributed in the United States by:
Publishers   Orca Book Publishers
35 Britain Street   P.O. Box 468
Toronto, Ontario   Custer, WA USA
M5A 1R7   98240–0468

Printed and bound in Canada.

Contents

For Meredith Bragg, who wanted a basketball story.

Acknowledgements

Thanks are due to Rob Driscoll, for lending his expertise in the sport of basketball and for checking this manuscript for accuracy, to my mother, Gail Martin, for her support and willingness to babysit during deadlines, and to my editor, Diane Young, for her insightful suggestions, enthusiasm, and professionalism.

1

The Queen of Cool

"What do you think?" I surveyed myself in the school's bathroom mirror.

"It's certainly ... uh ... different," said Taylor Anne Spence.

I smiled at myself. Today was our first day in grade eight, and I wanted to look special. My wraparound navy blue miniskirt reached to the middle of my thighs, and the sleek, cropped tank top showed off my stomach, which lay nice and flat, thanks to zero breakfast this morning. But best of all, the see-through navy chiffon blouse over it all billowed and floated at my every move. It was like being a movie star. I felt glamorous. I felt in control. If this outfit didn't make me stand out, I didn't know what would.

"Okay, let's go." I scooped up my books from the counter. "It's almost time for the bell." We slipped out into the hall just as the bell rang. Students poured through the doors in a flood, and we scurried ahead of the crowd toward our new homerooms. Taylor Anne and Chelsea Owens, my two best friends, were in different rooms this year. Amy Sehlmeier was in my homeroom, but considering the fact that we had hardly spoken since the Valentine's dance last year, I couldn't really count her as a friend.

Taylor Anne waved goodbye from the door of her classroom, and I hurried down the hall, feeling suddenly self-conscious and a little bit alone. I paused in the doorway when I found my class, and the kids who were already inside stopped scrambling for desks and stared. My teacher — this year I had Mrs. Kilton for homeroom — looked up, and her expression went blank.

I tugged at the hem of my skirt. "Um, hello," I said.

"Good morning, Kallana," Mrs. Kilton answered. "Go ahead and find a desk."

I slid into the nearest one, even though I knew it was uncool to sit in front by the teacher. I held my head up, but I felt uncomfortable.

Amy came in, wearing jeans with a hole in one knee and a rose-coloured sweatshirt, her long blond hair hanging down her back in a soft braid. Amy is one of those pixie-cute girls — small, athletic, and beautiful no matter what she does. I'm not. I'm tall, gangly, and awkward, with a face only a pit bull could love. I know it. My friends try to tell me I'm attractive, which is a lame word you use for someone when "pretty" doesn't apply. My mother, who runs a modelling agency, tells me I'm "interesting." But I know the truth. I see it every time I look in the mirror. I'm completely ugly. My nose is too big. My eyes are blah-grey, and they're too small and narrow-set. My lips are thin, my chin is blunt, my hair is yellow — not gold — and as stiff and straight as straw ... I could go on and on. Sometimes I wonder if someone who was ugly as a kid could grow up to be fantastically beautiful, but when I look at myself, I doubt it. I'd need plastic surgery on every major feature.

Sometimes wearing funky clothes makes me feel almost good-looking. Most of the other girls don't have expensive wardrobes, but my mom lets me pick out whatever I want. She doesn't mind what I spend. I fingered the delicate chiffon on my shirt and immediately felt better. *It* certainly was beautiful.

Mrs. Kilton said all the usual first-day stuff, including asking us if we'd had a good summer. I didn't even pretend to answer, while the rest of the class, it seemed, shouted, "Yes!"

My summer couldn't have been much worse if I'd sat down and planned it that way. My dad, who had promised to take my mom and me on a two-week vacation to California, had to cancel the trip because he got booked for a big job with *Canadian Nature Digest*. He's a freelance photographer, and he'd been waiting for this assignment for nearly six months. Still, it didn't seem fair that they could just suddenly decide to go ahead with a photographic layout of swamp bugs. Yes, swamp bugs. Dad explained the type of insect in great detail to me and told me why an article on this bug was so fascinating, but I still didn't get it. What I did get was the message that since this particular swamp bug was not fond of autumn or winter, this job had to be done during the summer, which meant our trip was off.

So I didn't get to go to Disneyland, I didn't get to see Universal Studios, and I didn't get to walk down Hollywood Boulevard. But I did get to spend the entire summer in the same house with my mother, while my dad was out of town for nearly two months.

And that's the other reason why I had a horrible summer. My mother is not exactly kid-friendly. At least, not to me, her own daughter. If I were a five-year-old cutesy-pie who could do commercials, had a portfolio of good black-and-white photographs, and had experience in catalogue modelling, I'm sure she'd love me better. But because I'm plain (very plain) old Kallana, just the daughter in the next room, she pretty much ignores me. Sometimes I think she wishes I'd just disappear — maybe go off to boarding school or college, so she could concentrate on her dumb business.

So, except for spending some time at the mall with my friends, I considered the summer before grade eight a write-off.

"Ms. Ohlmstead?" Mrs. Kilton was frowning at me. "I hope it's not too much trouble to ask you to pay attention on the first day of school, but I'd like you to come up here and sign out your textbook, please."

My cheeks grew warm. I saw that about half of the class had their texts. Mrs. Kilton, who was also going to be our teacher for social studies again this year, had probably been calling kids up from the class list, and had reached the Os without me hearing her.

I stood up and tugged at my skirt again. It felt awfully short, almost as though there was nothing covering my legs at all. I saw Mrs. Kilton's eyes shift over my top, then down to my knees, and her lips tightened.

My face felt hotter. I had liked Mrs. Kilton's class last year, even if I hadn't always acted like it, and this didn't seem like a good way to start off a new year. I wondered if she remembered all the times she caught me whispering in class with Taylor Anne and Chelsea and Amy. I wondered if she remembered the time I didn't work on my group project and read fashion magazines instead. I stole a quick look at her face.

She remembered.

She gave me a stare like I was a bug she'd like to brush off her desk and handed me my text. "Write your name on this sheet, and the number of the book. The number is written on the back-cover flap in black felt pen."

She went on calling out names, and one by one, the rest of the class came up to her desk. I signed my name quickly, wrote down the number 42, and slid quickly back into my desk.

When Mrs. Kilton had finished with the textbooks, she stood up and looked at the clock. "All right, kids. I'm sure your parents have told you how our timetable will work for the first day, but I'll repeat it just in case."

Good, I thought. Because I don't think Mom even opened that stuff the school mailed out.

"We have started with homeroom, followed by whatever class your homeroom teacher teaches for a twenty-minute period. In our case, that is social studies, so we have just had that class for today. You will move on to math next, then science, language arts, and phys. ed. Each period for the rest of the day will be only twenty minutes long. You will not be going to your options classes today. Those will start tomorrow, when we begin our regular schedule. You will come back to this room after your last class, before we have early dismissal at 11:45. Those of you who take the bus must be outside the school before twelve noon to catch your bus home. Everybody understand? I'm passing out your schedules now so you'll know which teacher you have for each class. As of tomorrow, we will be following this."

I glanced over the sheet of paper Mrs. Kilton placed on my desk, then shoved it in my backpack. I was more worried about showing up at home at lunchtime, when my family didn't expect me until 3:30. I hoped Mom was home. I didn't have a key.

"You may go to your math classroom now," Mrs. Kilton said, just as the bell rang through the hallway.

I felt Mrs. Kilton's gaze on me as I left the classroom, and it made me feel uncomfortable. It was that way for the rest of the morning — even though my friends thought my outfit was incredibly cool, the teachers all acted like I looked strange, like I'd turned up in my nightgown or something. By the time I got back to homeroom, I was pretty tired of it.

Mrs. Kilton asked us how our classes went, and I stared out the window without hearing what anyone said. It was only when the bell rang and I stood up that Mrs. Kilton focused on me.

"Kallana, stay behind for a moment, will you?"

"But I have to catch my bus."

"It'll just take a minute."

I rolled my eyes at Taylor Anne and Chelsea, who were waiting for me just outside the classroom door. They gave me sympathetic grins and motioned that they would wait in the hall.

Mrs. Kilton took a white envelope from the top of her desk. "I'd like you to give this to your mother or father, Kallana, and have one of them sign it before you bring it back."

"What for?" I asked.

Mrs. Kilton frowned. "You'll see when your parents have a chance to read it."

"Am I in trouble? It's only the first day of school."

"You're not in trouble, dear. Now hurry before your bus leaves."

It was my turn to frown. Notes are not usually sent home for signatures unless a kid is in trouble. And I didn't like the way Mrs. Kilton wouldn't tell me what the note was about. It obviously concerned me — didn't I have a right to know what it was about?

But I did have to catch my bus, and Taylor Anne was waiting with Chelsea. I turned on my heel and walked out the door.

Taylor Anne pounced on me the second I walked into the hall. "What did she want?"

"She gave me a note for home."

"What for?"

I shrugged. "Don't know." I made my voice cold. I didn't want to hear any more questions.

I saw Taylor Anne and Chelsea give each other a meaning-ful glance, like they knew that I knew more than I was telling. But I didn't. Know anything, that is.

But I was going to. Once I was safely on the bus, I meant to open the note. Mom wouldn't guess that it had come in an envelope — she hardly looked at this type of thing, anyway.

First, though, I had to put up with Taylor and Chelsea giggling about dumb things, like how Kyle Javer looked in his new jeans, and whether Jennie Brewster was dyeing her hair darker. As soon as they left to catch their own bus — they lived in a different district than I did — I pulled the envelope out of my pocket and slit it open with my thumb.

Dear Mr. or Mrs. Ohlmstead,
I would like to advise you that the clothing Kallana chose to wear today is considered inappropriate for junior high school. While we don't enforce a strict dress code, unusually revealing or provocative cloth-ing is discouraged. In the future, if Kallana insists upon wearing this type of clothing to school, she will be asked to change, or will be sent home to do so.
I just wanted to make you aware of the situation.
Sincerely,
Elaine Kilton

Blood rushed to my face, and my skin tingled with shame. Inappropriate? I extended my arm and stared at the beautiful, sheer chiffon of my blouse. Provocative? I mean, nothing was showing — it's not like you could see my bra or my under-wear. The skirt was a little short, I guess. And the tank top underneath was shaped a little like a sports bra — but did showing your belly button count as provocative? What exactly did *provocative* mean? This outfit looked exactly like the feature fashion spread in the last issue of *Teen Scene*. It was hip and sexy, sure. But provocative, no way.

I wondered what Mom would say. When I brought the outfit home from the store, she'd barely looked at it. She just nodded and said the colour was nice. Would she be mad?

In a way, I kind of hoped so. She'd *have* to notice me then, even if it was for something bad. It was embarrassing, though. I'd bought this outfit because it was so cool, like something you'd see on T.V. I thought it would make my friends notice me, maybe even make me look beautiful.

Instead, all it did was get me a note sent home from school.

2

Introducing Supermom

The bus dropped me off two blocks from my house. Only three other kids got off with me, and I didn't know any of them. The two girls looked like seventh graders, and the boy had to be in grade nine — he was probably new, since I hadn't ridden with him at all last year.

I live in Cottonwood Heights, a new district along the west edge of Calgary. The houses are big, with either pale stucco or brick finishes, and they all have mountain views, which is supposed to be impressive, but I don't get why adults seem to like looking at those piles of rocks.

We moved to this house four years ago, and it still feels too new and polished to be home. Except for my room. I managed to get my dad to agree to let me decorate it myself just after we moved in, and it's cozy and comfortable, even if I did get peach-coloured paint on the new baseboards.

I tried the door. It was unlocked, which meant someone — my mom, probably — was home. I kicked off my shoes, put the black leather satchel I used for my books down on the tile floor, and padded down the hallway in my nylons. I wanted to get this over with.

"Mom?" I eased open the french doors.

She swivelled in her office chair, tangling the phone cord around herself. She put one hand on the mouth of the receiver and raised her eyebrows. "What are you doing home?" she asked. Then, without waiting for an answer, she turned back to the phone. "No, I think I'd rather book her for a local job. Give her a little exposure before we try something like that. Yes, I have contacts in New York. No. No, she needs test shots and tearsheets before they'll look at her. Yes. Well, I think she may have potential, but it's impossible to tell until we get some black-and-whites of her. No, she doesn't have to take a modelling course to sign up with my agency. Yes, we do offer them. You'll have to check with the receptionist at our main office. She'll be glad to give you the information on upcoming courses. All right. Thank you for calling, Cathleen."

Mom hung up the phone, gave a hollow groan, and rubbed her temples. "Oh, how I loathe those modelling mothers! And why — why, after I tell Jayna down at the office to quit doing this, does she continue to put these calls through to me at home! I'm busy enough here without having to deal with a nagging mom who thinks her daughter is the next Supermodel of the Century." She looked at me. "Be glad that I'm conscientious enough never to embarrass you like that. The girls who walk in to see me with mothers like that always look so hangdog and resigned, as though they want to sink through the floor."

No, I thought. You'd never embarrass me by thinking I'm terrific. That has never happened. I eyed my mother — she was wearing a thin white cotton shirt and a long black skirt made of some stretchy, nubbly fabric. Work clothes.

"Going out to meet a client?" I asked.

"No. Just back." Mom sorted through some notes on her desk without looking up. I watched her. I wouldn't exactly say my mother is pretty, but there's something about her that makes people look at her. Everything is honed to perfection — the eyebrows are tweezed, the skin is polished, the makeup is artfully applied. The hair is always fashionably cut. Her eyes are steel grey and close-set like mine, but larger, with thicker lashes. Her nose is too long and too bony, and her chin is too narrow, I thought, glad to find something that wasn't quite perfect.

It would have been better if I'd looked like either Mom or Dad, but except for Mom's eye colour, I'm a mixture of unknown ancestors, and it came out awful. Dad has twinkly green eyes and black hair that's so fine it never looks neat — it ruffles up in spiky tufts the minute he puts his comb away. His face is narrow, too, but nicer, somehow, than mine. I think I'd have liked to look more like him.

"What's the matter?" Mom said abruptly, finishing with her notes and seeing me still standing there. "And why are you home? It's only lunchtime."

"It's a half day today. We don't start the regular schedule until tomorrow."

"Why don't they tell us these things! Suppose I wasn't home? If I had time, I'd call the school and complain."

"They did tell us. It came in the mail last week in an info-pack the school sent out. You never read it."

I expected her to flinch at my accusing tone, but she never even blinked. "Sending information out in an envelope that looks like junk mail is hardly a reliable way of distributing news."

"Hmmph." I plopped down in the overstuffed armchair that stood in one corner of the office. My skirt flew out in a brief, short fan, and I smoothed it carefully over my legs. "My teacher asked me to bring this home." I casually tossed the note on her desk. I knew she would ignore it, but I also knew Mrs. Kilton would get on my case if I didn't bring it back with Mom's signature, so I persevered. "She wants you to sign it, so I can bring it back."

"Hmm? Okay." Mom reached for the note, her eyes on the sheaf of black-and-white photographs she had just pulled from an envelope. She unfolded the note, gave it a cursory glance, and began to sign it. Then her eyes swept over the note a second time, and I held my breath.

"What? Is this teacher from the dark ages? What were you wearing today?"

"This." I gestured down the length of my body.

Mom eyed me. "It's suitable for the runway, but I guess it's a bit risqué for school. Still ... oh, well." Mom signed the note and handed it back to me. "Next time you wear that blouse, go for a full tank top underneath and wear some thick navy tights with that skirt." Then she turned and began dialling the phone.

I was left with the feeling of being dismissed, and I knew from experience that if I stayed in her office, Mom would get irritated at first, then extremely ticked off. I left, clutching the note, and went upstairs to my room. At least it welcomed me.

The peach walls gave the room a warm look, and my collection of stuffed animals on the bookshelf looked down at me with their friendly glass eyes. I sat down on the puffy, flowered comforter on the bed and stripped off my nylons. I pulled off the rest of my outfit and put on a pair of blue sweatpants and a fuzzy flannel shirt. The sweatpants had a grease stain on the knee, and the shirt didn't even remotely match — it was pink-and-green plaid. But the clothes were comfortable and soft, and could not possibly be criticized as provocative or revealing. I flopped down on my bed and, for some reason, felt unexplainably depressed.

* * *

Every day for the next two weeks I wore clothes that I thought were stylish, but that weren't especially *provocative*. I was beginning to hate that word. Every morning when I woke up and got dressed, I wondered what it really meant. Did it mean showing off your breasts? What if you hardly had breasts yet … did that count? Was it so wrong to dress like the models in magazines? Is wanting to look pretty a bad thing? Is sexy the same as provocative? I worried about it, but I had no idea what to do. I *needed* to be cool. What if the cool stuff was provocative, and Mrs. Kilton sent me home, in front of the whole class? That would be, like, minus twelve on the cool meter.

But by the end of October, I'd almost forgotten about it. Mrs. Kilton still looked at me funny when I wore my coolest stuff, but at least she wasn't making a big deal out of it. So I wasn't completely prepared on the Monday morning our phys. ed. teacher stopped me. I was wearing this really feminine, floaty pink dress with a matching baby cardigan sweater. The incident with Mrs. Kilton came back in a flash.

"Kallana?" Ms. Wright came up to me in the cafeteria line, where I was standing with Chelsea and Taylor Anne.

"Yeah?" I said, a little panicky. Was she going to tell me that this outfit was provocative and revealing, too?

"How tall are you?"

"Huh?" I didn't expect this question at all. "Um … maybe 5'7" or so."

"Really? You look taller than that. I would have guessed you were about 5'9"."

Oh, great. Did she have to bring up the subject of my geeky overgrowth in front of everyone? "Well, uh … I could be. I haven't been measured in a while."

"Oh. Well, listen. I think I'll have a few openings on the Grizzlies junior girls' basketball team. Practice starts in a few weeks. You might do really well. You have the height, and I bet you can handle a ball pretty well."

I swallowed as Chelsea and Taylor Anne tried to stifle their giggles. "I'm really not into sports much," I said as politely as I could. Squat and thickly muscled, Ms. Wright looked like she did nothing *but* excercise.

"You should think about it, Kallana. We could really use you. And it would be a great learning experience."

"I don't think so," I said, my voice laced with the faintest tinge of sarcasm. "But thanks anyway."

Ms. Wright gave me a sorrowful look. "All right. If you change your mind ...." She walked away.

"Not in this lifetime," I said under my breath. Chelsea and Taylor Anne collapsed against each other, choking on their laughter.

"Can you imagine Kallana playing basketball?" Chelsea gasped. "The only thing funnier would be Mrs. Kilton doing the hula!"

Taylor Anne snorted. "What about her in one of those baggy old uniforms? She'd rather die!"

I stayed silent. Was I really that much of a sports loser? I supposed it was better this way. A person just couldn't look trendy and sweaty at the same time.

We moved up the line, where Taylor Anne chose a package of potato chips and ordered a pizza pop and a can of cola from the lunch lady behind the counter.

"Is that all you're having?" Taylor said when I asked for a diet pop and a container of yoghurt.

"I have an orange with me," I said. "You have to watch what you eat if you want to stay model thin." I looked at her pointedly. Taylor Anne had asked my mother a few months ago if she could get into modelling, and Mom had told her to wait a year or so to see how her bones developed. Taylor is totally pretty. She has glossy brown hair, straight teeth, and a nice complexion, but she looks more like the cheerleader type than the strong-boned, austere type that is the rage in modelling right now. At least, that's what my mother told me afterwards. Her words, exactly.

I knew I was being mean, reminding Taylor of that, but I didn't like being laughed at. Was it really such a joke, the idea of me playing basketball? I mean, I knew it was, but it sort of hurt, the way they laughed about it.

Taylor Anne blushed and put back the bag of potato chips. "That's all," she said to the lunch lady, paying her for the pizza pop, which had just been microwaved and was steaming on a paper plate. It smelled good, and I half-wished I'd gotten one, too.

Chelsea looked a bit annoyed. She's verging on plump, but she likes junk food too much to stop eating it. "Well, *I* don't want to be a model," she said. She put some taco chips and a chocolate bar on the counter and ordered a pizza pop, a chocolate-chip muffin, and a can of root beer.

I know this doesn't sound like regular cafeteria food, but our school doesn't really have one any more. We used to, but all we have now is a little booth at the back of the lunchroom, where you can buy candy, pop, chips, muffins, yoghurt, milk, pizza pops, and stale sandwiches. That's it. Finito. No good ol' sloppy joes or meatloaf here. Not that I really mind, but on the almost-every-day days when I forget to make my lunch, I kind of wish I had more variety to choose from.

The three of us moved toward a table and sat down. I could see Amy Sehlmeier, my ex-friend, joking and laughing with Jennie Brewster and Kyle Javer. They looked like they were having a riot, and I kind of wished Amy and I were friends again. She was the only girl I knew who cared about more than clothes and makeup and looking pretty. Amy and Jennie are both competitive figure skaters, which is kind of interesting. I'd never said that to them, though. Sports aren't my thing.

I turned my back. I'd never be an athlete. If there was one thing that Kallana Ohlmstead would never, ever do, it was sweat in public.

3

Dad Decides

October turned into November. I was sitting at the kitchen table with my mom and dad, eating supper a few weeks later, chewing and staring off into space. The kitchen lights, which were turned on against the early darkness, glared against the stark white cabinets and gleaming counter tops. I like softer, traditional decorating, but my mother is into modern, and I felt like I had to squint against the brightness in the kitchen. I speared a piece of tomato with my fork and tried to ignore the feeling that I was eating in a laboratory.

Chelsea and I had spent the afternoon at the mall, trying on shoes and wandering around. I was deciding whether to go back the next day for the brown leather boots or a pair of black shoes that looked like ballet slippers. I was mentally going through my clothes to see what I would wear with the shoes, when my dad spoke to me.

"Kallie? I saw your teachers today."

I nearly choked on a mouthful of salad. "You did? Why?"

"We had parent-teacher interviews. Didn't you bother to wonder why you had a holiday this afternoon?" Dad grinned at me.

I swallowed. "No, I just went with it."

"Of course. Well, I was impressed. They all seemed pretty good. I liked Mrs. Kilton. I think you're lucky to have her."

Mom, who was immersed in the news on the portable television on our kitchen counter, roused herself to give a snort. "That depends. She sent me a note on the first day of school criticizing how Kallana dressed. I'd call that pretty intolerant."

Dad eyed Mom. "What was she wearing? And why didn't you tell me about it?"

"I did. You just never listen." Mom focused back on the newscaster. "Shhh, I want to hear this."

Dad turned back to me. "What were you wearing?"

I felt my cheeks turn pink. "I … uh, well, I'll show you later. Just a skirt and a blouse with a tank top. But Mrs. Kilton said it was provocative."

I felt Dad's steady gaze on me. "I know how much you like to fool around with clothes, Kallie, but school isn't the place to pretend you're on a Paris runway."

"I know, Dad." I suppressed a sigh.

"Anyway, that's not what I want to talk about. I happened to talk to the teacher who is coaching girls' basketball this year. She told me she asked you to play."

I gave a half-shrug.

"Did she ask you, Kallana?"

"Yes."

"What did you say?"

"I said no." I glanced up and saw Dad's eyebrows narrowed into a crease. "I was polite — there's no reason to look at me like that."

"Do you realize what a compliment it is to be asked to play on the team, without even having to try out? That coach obviously thinks you've got talent."

No, what the coach has is not enough players, I thought. She's desperate, especially if she's asking me. But I didn't say anything.

"Kallie, playing basketball would be great. It's a lot of fun, and you'll get to meet some new friends."

"Dad, I have my own friends already. And I'm just not into basketball, okay?"

"I'd like to see you develop some other interests besides spending your mother's money on trendy clothes and trying to mould yourself into some fashion editor's idea of female beauty. There's a whole world out there of interesting things, and you sit here and try to be a Barbie doll. I don't like it, Kallie. I mean, I understand that some of this is a normal part of becoming a teenager, but I want you to get out and have a good time, without worrying about how you look for a change."

"Dad, this isn't some deep psychological thing, okay? I just don't want to play basketball."

"Well, I guess that's too bad, because I told the coach you'd be there for practice tomorrow after school."

"You did what?" I shrieked. "Dad, how could you? That's totally not fair! I'm not going."

"Yes, you are."

"No, I'm not!"

"Oh yes, you are."

"No, I'M NOT!"

"Would you two quiet down?" Mom said irritably, turning up the volume. "I can't hear the news."

I positively glared at my mother, so hard I thought my eyeballs were actually bulging. "I don't care whether you can hear the news! I am not playing basketball! NOT EVER!" I shoved back my chair and stomped toward the stairs.

"This discussion isn't finished, Kallana," my dad said.

"It is for me!" I ran up to my room and slammed the door. I stood there, glowering for a minute, imagining all the awful things that would happen to me if my dad made me play basketball. I'd look even uglier than usual, with my hair all

sweaty and tied back any old way. The uniforms were hideous
— green and white with yellow trim and baggy all over. I'd
make a complete idiot out of myself, because I could hardly
even bounce the ball. I didn't know the rules — I'd make
stupid mistakes in front of everyone. My friends would come
to watch me and they'd laugh. The whole school would laugh.
The entire universe would laugh.

I realized I could hear shouting downstairs, and I opened
my door a crack.

"Why couldn't you go to parent-teacher interviews, Lydia? Give me one good reason." My dad's voice sounded tight
with anger.

"Because I had meetings all afternoon with clients, that's
why. And don't start playing the heavy parent role with me,
Greg. You haven't bothered to go to those school functions
since the day Kallana started kindergarten."

"If I was in town, I made the effort."

"Oh yes. If you were in town. If it was convenient."
Mom's voice was syrupy-sarcastic, then turned as cold and
brittle as ice. "Don't guilt trip me, Greg. I've been to Kallana's interviews and pageants and Christmas concerts alone
more times than I can count. Why is it that if you can't go to
your daughter's school functions because of work, that's
okay, but if I can't, it's just an excuse?"

"It isn't … "

"Oh yes, it is. And let me tell you, I'm tired of waiting
around for my career to happen. And I'm especially tired of
waiting for yours to happen."

"Let's not get into that."

"Oh no, let's not. At least, not until the mortgage is due, or
the next car payment. Or the next instalment on that ob-
scenely expensive camera you just bought."

"Lyd, stop it."

"I don't want to stop. You're never home, and you never want to talk when you are home. Don't you see, Greg?"

I listened hard, but I couldn't hear any more. Either they were whispering, or they were hugging. I hoped they were hugging.

I felt guilty. Was it my fault? If I hadn't thrown a fit about the basketball team, would my parents have just sat together and watched the news as usual? Had I caused that fight? I'd never heard my mother sound so angry before. This wasn't a yelling, you-broke-my-new-lipstick kind of anger, but a hard, cold anger that made me shiver, and I felt scared.

I don't know how long I'd been sitting on the edge of my bed, staring at nothing, when my father tapped lightly on my door.

"Can I come in?" he asked.

"Yes," I said.

"Kallie, I'm sorry if you don't like the idea, but I'd really be proud if you gave the team a try."

"Why?"

"Because I think you'd surprise yourself — I think you're a lot more talented than you give yourself credit for."

"Hah."

"And because there's a person inside Kallana Ohlmstead that is a lot more than trendy outfits and new hairstyles, and I'd like the world to get to know her."

"Double hah." My throat suddenly closed.

"Why do you say that?" Dad regarded me steadily.

"Because how you look *does* matter. And it's stupid to pretend that it doesn't. You're saying that there's more to me on my inside than other people see, but that makes me want to laugh. Do you think that Mom would ever ask me to be one of her models? Have you ever asked to photograph me for one of your ad layouts? No! And why? Because I'm not pretty. Even worse, I'm ugly."

"Kall, you're not ugly."

"Yes, I am. And what's more, if I didn't wear the best outfits and do my hair really cool, I'd be one of the ugliest girls in my school."

"Now you're exaggerating."

Why do parents always say that? "I am not."

"And what's inside *does* count. Even if other people can't see it, you can."

Tears prickled my eyelids. "I don't want to talk about it any more."

"Fine. But you are going to basketball practice tomorrow afternoon. I expect to hear all about it."

I could only nod, my eyes tightly closed. I would have made a fuss, except I knew Dad was immovable, and I felt suddenly tired. I didn't want to start another argument between Mom and Dad, either. So I nodded stiffly and drew my knees up to my chest. I pressed my forehead into my knees, and I sat there for a long time, not moving, even after Dad gave my shoulder an encouraging squeeze and left the room.

4

Kallana the Athlete

The toilet stall was damp, clammy, and smelled like old sweat socks, but it was better than going out there. I could hear the other girls in the locker-room talking, laughing, slamming the metal doors shut.

I leaned against the door of my stall, holding my breath. My hands wouldn't stop shaking, and a cold ache had settled in the pit of my stomach. I couldn't go out there. I just couldn't.

I waited until all the girls had gone, then I silently unlatched the door and crept out. I had no uniform, so I changed into my gym clothes. I pulled the hairpins from my hair, which held my long bangs back in a behind-the-ears tucked style, and combed out the hairspray. Then I pinned my bangs back with a barrette — the rest of my hair was too short for a ponytail — and looked at myself in the mirror. A pale girl with chalky skin and scared grey eyes stared back. There was nothing of the sophisticated Kallana Ohlmstead I'd tried to show the world. Only a scared grade-eight girl, who couldn't shoot a basketball if her life depended on it!

I walked slowly up the stairs — our phys. ed. lockers were located in the lower level of the school — until I got to the hallway in front of the gym. I heard the screech of sneakers against the varnished floor and the rhythmic thudding of basketballs up and down the gym. Occasionally there was a smacking noise, as though a ball had hit a wall.

"Good job, Jane. Use the backboard. Again! Again!" Ms. Wright's voice rang out over the other sounds.

I took a deep breath and walked into the gym. At first no one noticed me. They all kept running around, tossing balls back and forth, leaping for the hoop. It looked extremely disorganized, but I guess they knew what they were doing, because nobody seemed to be confused except me. One or two of the girls caught sight of me, and I saw them nudge their nearest neighbour with an elbow. Gradually, the gym grew quiet, and Ms. Wright looked up to find out what was wrong. When she saw me standing there in the gym doorway, she put a big smile on her face.

"Kallana! Glad you came." She pushed a lock of her cropped brown hair off her forehead. "Girls, I'm sure you know one another, but this is Kallana Ohlmstead, and she's going to be joining our team this season."

This was greeted with a bunch of blank looks. One or two girls covered their mouths with their hands to hide a snicker. I braced myself. I had known this was coming.

"Kallana, why don't you go with that group over there. We're working on lay-ups and passing drills. Just follow along as best you can. The girls will help you out."

Sure they will, I thought. I walked over to the group she had pointed out. Five other girls eyed me with the same enthusiasm they'd give a wad of gum stuck to their shoe. Jane Evans was one of them — she was a girl who hung out sometimes with Jennie Brewster and Amy. She was the ultimate jock type — short brown hair, boys' clothes, square build, muscular. I winced inwardly as I realized Jane was one of the girls I'd labelled a *jeek* last year with my friends, meaning a cross between a geek and a jock. I wondered if she remembered.

I caught her staring, a slight smirk on her face. She remembered.

The only other girl in the group I knew was an eighth grader named Marty Cassella, and I didn't know her well. The others were in grade seven.

"Uh … hi," I said.

"Hi," said one of the seventh graders. "Want to go first?" She started to hand me a ball.

"Oh no. That's okay. You go." I had no idea what lay-ups and passing drills were.

"No, let Kallana go," Jane said, a wicked grin on her face. She gave me the ball. "Just dribble it —" She caught my blank expression. "— that's bouncing it, over to the hoop, do a jump, and try and get it in the basket."

I looked at the ball in my hands. There didn't seem to be any way to get out of this, so I said, "Okay." I began to bounce the ball slowly toward the basket.

"Faster," Jane called.

Fumbling, I tried to run and bounce at the same time. Just as I was about to jump, the ball bounced against my foot and skittered toward the wall. I chased it, embarrassed, because the girls all stopped to look.

"That's okay, Kallana. Just try it again," Ms. Wright called.

I groaned inwardly. Again? I just wanted to go home. But I started over, making a slow half circle toward the basket. This time I managed to get underneath the hoop, give a feeble little hop, and toss the ball toward the metal rim. It bounced off awkwardly, and I had to chase it again.

Ms. Wright walked over. "Not bad, Kallana. Watch Jane give it try, and I'll explain what you do, okay? All right. See how she keeps the rhythm going with her right hand? Now watch. She dribbles up, takes off from her left foot, and shoots with her right hand."

Jane made a smooth transition from running with the ball bouncing in front of her to leaping high in the air, the ball poised in one hand. She flipped it into the air, and the ball wobbled briefly on the rim before it tipped in with a soft whoosh.

"Nice work, Janie. Next time try to be more decisive when you put the ball in. Let it know who's boss." Ms. Wright grinned at her.

Jane jogged back to line up in our group, and the rest of the girls looked at me expectantly.

"Ready to try it?" Ms. Wright beckoned to one of the girls to throw her a ball.

"Again?" I squeaked. I'd been hoping not to.

"Yes. Just take it nice and easy. No one's expecting you to be perfect."

I took the ball from her, feeling the firm rubber between my palms. I walked over to the front of the line and bounced the ball a few times, just to get the feel of it. I wished everyone would stop watching.

I began to run, loping along with the ball. Just before I reached the hoop, I glanced upward and jumped. The ball sailed off my hand, and to my shock, headed straight for the basket. It hit the edge of the rim and circled around and around and around while I held my breath. Then it fell through the hoop and bounced with a *thunk!* on the gym floor.

I stood frozen with surprise. I'd actually made a basket! Ms. Wright clapped her hands enthusiastically, but Jane and the others looked bored. They didn't seem to appreciate the minor miracle that had just occurred.

As I jogged back to my place in line, I could feel myself beaming. Who would have believed that I could actually do it?

"Nice one," Jane commented. "Think you can do it again, instead of by accident?"

The pleasure of the moment seemed to drain out of me. But I had no answer. It *had* been an accident. A lucky fluke.

I turned my back. Even though I did five more lay-ups during the drill, not one went in. I tried to stay at the back of the line, but Jane kept pushing me forward, giving me pointers at the top of her lungs, so everyone was looking at me. She wasn't fooling me — she wasn't really trying to help. She was making sure I stayed embarrassed, and she enjoyed every minute.

Jerk, I thought angrily. I half-wished I'd never teased Jane before, because then maybe she would have left me alone. For the rest of the practice I counted the minutes until the coach called out that it was time to stop. Then I thought the worst was over.

I couldn't have been more wrong.

"All right, girls. Good practice today," Ms. Wright said. "I want all of you here right after dismissal tomorrow to warm up for the game, since it starts at 3:45. The team from Sponnick Junior High is a tough one, so we need to be ready. Uniforms on, hair tied back, clean socks. I want our team to look organized, ready to fight. Got it?"

I didn't. She'd lost me back around the words tomorrow and game. A real game? As in basketball? Tomorrow? But I'd had only one practice. I could barely tie up my running shoes properly, and she was already throwing me into a game?

But as I swallowed hard, I saw Jane looking at me out of the corner of her eye, and I wondered if the Sponnick team might be a bunch of pussycats next to my own team-mates.

5

On the Court

In class the next day, when the dismissal bell pealed through the halls, the personality of the entire class changed. The blankness disappeared, and everyone jumped out of their desks like coiled springs that had been let go.

Except for me.

Oh, man. I just couldn't face this. Why hadn't I thrown the flaming fit to end all fits with my dad? Why had I ever agreed to try basketball? In less than thirty minutes, I would face certain destruction, or at least humiliation, in that gym.

My math teacher was looking at me strangely. "Do you feel all right, Kallana?" she asked. I hadn't moved from my desk — not even budged.

That was a thought. I wondered if I could fake sick. But then Mom and Dad would have to be fooled at home, too. I doubted that there was such a thing as a two-hour flu.

"Yes, I'm okay." I heaved myself from the desk and trudged out into the hall. I had to leave my books in my locker, go to the gym and pick up my uniform, then get changed downstairs. If I didn't rush, I'd be late, but my legs just wouldn't obey. They walked slower and slower. My lock opened easily, in spite of me getting the combination just a little off. I tried to delay a little longer by stuffing my books in all helter-skelter, hoping they'd fall out and give me a little time while I scooped them up. But they stayed in.

Everything was conspiring against me. Any other time, my lock would refuse to open, my books would fall out, my shoes would come untied, and the janitor would be waxing the gym floor. But because I could not and absolutely would not play this basketball game, nothing stopped me.

Ms. Wright was waiting at the gym door. "Hurry, Kallana. I want to give you a chance to warm up, too, even though you won't get much game time today."

I felt my spirits lifting. "I won't?"

"I'm really sorry. But you just haven't had enough time to go over all the points of the game. And I've got a strong starter for the position I'm considering you for."

"Position?"

"Yes. I train everybody to play more than one, so they can get as much game time as possible, so you'll be given another one as well, but to start I think I'll put you in as centre. You're the tallest girl on the team, and I think you'd do well in that position."

"Oh. Sure." I had no idea what the centre did. All I cared about was the fact that I wouldn't actually have to play in today's game, after all.

"Here's your uniform." Ms. Wright plucked a jersey and a pair of shorts off the bleachers and handed them to me. "Go get changed. We need your support, and you might get a few minutes of playing time at the end. We'll see how the game goes."

"Oh no, that's all right," I said hurriedly. "I understand. I'll play another time." Like in ten years would be good, I thought. I backed away, clutching the green, white, and yellow uniform. It was slippery nylon and had a vague smell of sweat, dust, and fabric softener. I ran down the stairs to the gym locker-rooms in the basement, relief making me swift. I didn't have to play! Or at least, probably not. I felt like a weight had just dropped off my shoulders.

The rest of the girls were almost ready. They were laughing and chattering, hardly noticing me when I slipped inside. I twirled the combination on my lock, flipped it open, and tossed the uniform on the bench. Then I began to pull off my layers of clothes. It had been cold that morning, so I'd decided to wear my thick black tights with my ankle-length, rust brown skirt, a cream ribbed turtleneck, and my forest green wool blazer. I had on my black loafers with the big heels, and a black wool tam to wear outside with my coat. I would have taken it off inside, except that when I did, my hair looked like a porcupine on a bad-hair day, so I had kept it on.

I pulled all this stuff off and piled it on the bench. A few things fell off when I began pulling out my gym clothes, too. I had a pair of tennis shoes in my locker, two sets of shorts, three T-shirts, and my running shoes. I yanked them out, then began rummaging for clean socks. There were at least three pairs of dirty ones, but I knew there was a clean pair in there somewhere. When I found them, I put the running shoes, socks, and my uniform on the floor and gathered up all the rest of my junk and jammed it into my locker, shutting the door before anything could spill out. Then I pulled the uniform shirt over my head, tugged up the baggy shorts, put on my socks, and laced my running shoes.

Once I was sitting on the bench, tying my shoelaces, Jane came over, looked under the bench, then opened her locker.

"Did you see my sneakers?" she asked me suspiciously. "I left them right here while I went to brush my teeth, and now they're gone."

"Brush your teeth?" Under normal circumstances, this would have been a great time to make Jane feel like a dork, but as of yesterday, I didn't want to make things more difficult between us.

She gave me a metal-rimmed grimace. "Braces."

"Oh." I stood up. "I didn't see your shoes. Sorry." I left her there, frowning at the bench.

When I went upstairs, the gym had changed. It was filled with girls running, the rhythmic thudding of basketballs on the wood floor, and ski jackets thrown over the bleachers. Parents and teachers were finding seats and chatting with one another. Some of the teachers were from the other school, but most were from Meadowpark, there to support our team. Ms. Wright had lugged in a big thermos and was busy mixing drink crystals with water.

The team from Sponnick Junior High was dressed in red, with yellow and white trim. If it was possible, their uniforms looked even worse than ours. One girl on their team was very tall. She had red hair, and I just knew instantly, looking at her, that my mother would think she was fantastic. Maybe not supermodel material, but she had that model quality. Not a prettiness exactly, but something eye-catching about her face. I'd looked at enough model photos to tell. And it was funny — I didn't even know this girl, but I couldn't suppress a sinking feeling of jealousy, and a gladness that my mother cared so little about what I did that she'd never show up at one of my basketball games. I felt like it would be the height of public embarrassment if my mother walked up to that girl, in front of everyone, and asked her if she wanted to be a model. And if my mother ever saw that girl, that's exactly what would happen. Then everyone would look at me and ask, "So what's the matter with you? Why doesn't your mother want *you* to model?" And then I'd want to die.

"Kallana? Want to help me set up the paper cups?" Ms. Wright interrupted my thoughts.

"Sure." I reached for the stack of paper cups and began setting them out on the table beside the bleachers.

"Fill them part way, first. It's for half-time, so the girls don't have to wait for a drink. Then we'll mix some more to have after the game."

"Oh, okay." I held a paper cup underneath the spout. As we filled them, I felt more and more relaxed. This might be fun. I enjoyed the importance of placing the paper cups in rows along the table. I was admiring my work, when Jane came rushing up in her sock feet, her uniform jersey untucked, her eyes wild and panicked.

"Coach! I can't find my running shoes! I've looked all over the locker-room, and they're gone!"

Ms. Wright shook her head. "Jane, not again! Last week it was your uniform shorts you left at home in the laundry, and I remember distinctly that you lost three kneepads during volleyball season. If you don't start keeping track of your equipment, you'll lose so much that you'll be out here playing in your underwear."

Jane flushed. "But I had them, I swear. Someone must have taken them."

"Who would want to take shoes?" I asked.

Jane frowned at me.

"Kallana's right, Jane. Nobody would want to take your running shoes," Ms. Wright said.

"Especially if they got close enough to smell them," I muttered. I couldn't help it — the words were just asking to be said. Jane really glared at me this time, but Ms. Wright pretended she hadn't heard.

"They must be around somewhere, unless you left them at home."

"I didn't." Jane looked around, as though she hoped her sneakers would suddenly appear from under the bleachers.

"Well, if you don't find them, Jane, you're going to have to sit out the game."

Jane blanched. *What?*

"You'll have to sit out the game. You can't play without running shoes."

"But I have to play!"

"Then you should have made sure you had a pair of shoes, don't you think?" Ms. Wright looked exasperated. "And Kallana, this means I'll have to put you in."

"*What?*" I felt my own face grow pale. "I can't!"

"You have to. You're the only other player I have for centre."

"But I don't even know how to play! I don't know all the rules!"

"I'll talk you through it as best I can. Unless Jane comes up with some sneakers, you're in."

I turned to Jane. "What size do you wear?"

"Seven. Why?"

I sighed. "Mine are nines. They're too big. Maybe someone else can lend you shoes."

"Like who?" Jane said bitterly. "Everyone else wants to play."

"Did you look in your locker?" I asked.

Jane snorted. "Of course. Do you think I'm a moron? That's the first place I checked."

I was silent. Obviously there was nothing I could say that would help, even if Jane and I were friends, which we definitely were not.

"Kallana, come over here, please." Ms. Wright beckoned to me from the bench, where she sat surrounded by the rest of the team. Jane remained where she was.

"Okay, Kallana. As the centre, you start the game with the tip-off. That means when the ref tosses the ball, you jump for it and try to tip the ball with your fingers toward one of our players, so we get possession. Okay?"

"Sure." I nodded, but I had almost no idea what the coach was talking about. Tip? Possession? The only thing I understood was that I had to jump for the ball, and I figured I could at least do that.

The referee blew her whistle, and the teams ran out onto the gym floor. Ms. Wright slapped my shoulder encouragingly, and I followed my team with my heart in my throat.

One of the girls pointed to where I was supposed to stand, and I took my position on the court. Then I saw who I was facing on the opposite team — the tall girl with red hair, the potential model. She smiled at me, but I felt my insides shrivel even more. Bad enough that I had to do this without my opponent looking like a magazine cover.

The referee tossed the ball in the air. I leaped, but I was too early. I came down before the ball reached my outstretched hand, and the redhead whapped it away. One of her team-mates got the ball and bounced it down the court. Everybody ran after her, so I ran, too. Our team tried to circle her to get the ball away, but she passed it to the redhead.

"Heads up, Daria!" she called. Redheaded Daria caught the ball neatly and pounded toward the basket.

"Kallana! Cover her!" Ms. Wright yelled from the sidelines. I dashed after Daria, but I had no idea what to do. When I tried to hit the ball away from her, Daria just sidestepped me, bouncing it against the floor. After a few futile tries, Daria brushed past me and flew toward the basket, leaping high and tossing the ball through the hoop.

"Yay! Way to go Daria!" The calls came from the bleachers, and a few of her team-mates slapped her hand. Again, I didn't know what to do, but I felt awful inside.

The referee beckoned to me and positioned me underneath the basket, outside the court lines, and handed me the ball. I looked at her questioningly.

"Throw it in," she said.

I shrugged and tossed the ball in. One of the other team's players scooped it up and ran toward the basket, sinking the ball with an easy lay-up. I heard Jane groan from the side-lines. I felt my face burn, but I didn't know what I'd done wrong. The ref *said* to throw it in.

Ms. Wright motioned for me to come over. "Kallana, next time make it a decisive pass. Get it right to one of our players — don't give them a chance to take it away."

"I can throw it to someone?" I asked. "The ref just told me to throw the ball in."

Jane rolled her eyes. "You're supposed to pass it to some-one, dummy. Preferably someone on your own team."

I looked down at the floor so Jane couldn't see my redden-ing face. I just knew playing basketball was a dumb idea. How was I supposed to know what to do?

"It's okay, Kallana. Go back in," Ms. Wright said.

I jogged back onto the court, my face hot. I avoided looking at anyone, and when Marty tossed the ball in to one of our players, I stuck close to Daria, covering her so she couldn't try to get the ball. That's all I could do, but Daria was a good player. She wormed away from me time after time, and once she was in the clear, someone always passed the ball to her. Then I had to scramble after her, while she scored basket after basket.

I'd never felt so completely humiliated in my entire life.

That is, until Marty passed me the ball. I didn't know what to do with it. I searched the sidelines for Ms. Wright, and she was waving her arms in the direction of the other team's basket. Right. That was obvious. I began dribbling the ball down the court, but just as I got close enough to take a shot, Daria swiped it from me, jostling me hard with her elbow at the same time.

Phweeet! The ref blew hard on her whistle, and everyone stopped.

"Foul!" she yelled. "Take the shot from the free-throw line." She handed the ball to me. The other players lined up along the keyhole-shaped line on the gym floor. The ref placed me at the top of the key, and told me to take two shots at the basket.

The gym was still. All the parents, teachers, and the rest of the teams were watching. The players were poised, ready to grab the ball after the rebound. Daria looked like a cat waiting to pounce.

I slowly raised the ball above my head. I looked at the basket, which seemed miles away. I'd never get the ball through that far-away hoop. I bent my knees and tried to get my hands around the ball, but my whole body was shaking. Everyone was staring at me. Nausea swelled in my throat. I had a sudden vision of myself throwing up on the gym floor in front of everyone, and I knew I couldn't do this.

I put my hands down. "I'm sorry. I can't," I whispered. And I walked off the court.

6

The Locker Disaster

I went straight to Ms. Wright and told her I felt sick, which was the truth. I had to endure Jane's sardonic eye. She might as well have yelled at the top of her lungs, "Baby!" I knew that was what she was thinking. Ms. Wright talked to the referee, and she let Marty take my place for the free throw, since Marty had to take my position as centre. That left us without a point guard, so Ms. Wright put in Traci Dharwani, one of the grade-seven girls that had been playing that position in practice.

It didn't matter. No one could be worse than me, and even though Traci was short and scared, she knew a lot more about basketball than I did. I sat on the bleachers and took some deep breaths. My hands gradually stopped shaking, and I tried to ignore the glances of the people around me. Jane wasn't so easy to ignore. She never missed an opportunity to scowl at me.

When the game finally ended — Score: Sponnick 52, Meadowpark 16 — relief flooded through me. I rushed down to the locker-room with the rest of the team to get changed. Jane tagged along with us, still in her sock feet and uniform. She hadn't bothered to change back, even after she found out she wouldn't be playing.

I spun the combination on my lock, with nothing on my mind except escape. My plan went no farther than getting dressed as fast as possible and running for the bus. I could shower at home.

I was completely unprepared for the avalanche of clothing that tumbled out of my locker. I'd forgotten how I'd shoved everything in, and now tights and socks and shoes rained down on the floor. I groaned inwardly, knelt on the floor, and began to pick up what I needed to wear. And at that moment, Jane looked down.

"My shoes!" she yelled.

I jumped. "What?"

"My shoes! You had my running shoes in your locker the whole time!" Jane snatched them up and held them to her chest as though they were made of gold.

I looked at them in bewilderment. "But I didn't —!"

"You did it on purpose, didn't you? So I couldn't play! I can't believe you, Kallana. You're a total witch!"

Hot anger began to boil inside me. "I never took your shoes, Jane," I said icily. "I don't know how they got in my locker, but I didn't put them there."

"Oh yeah, right. And you expect me to believe that?"

"It's the truth."

"You wouldn't know the truth if it jumped up and bit you on the rear."

I looked away. I'd endured more humiliation in the last hour than I ever had before in my life. I wouldn't be able to keep the tears back much longer. "I didn't take your shoes, Jane."

Jane glared. "I *saw* them fall out. Explain that!"

I shrugged. "I can't."

Jane began to gather up her clothes in quick, jerky movements. "You're a lying, stuck-up snot," she said, walking away. "And I *hate* you, Kallana."

"I hate you, too!" I yelled after her, as the locker-room door banged shut behind her. The other girls were standing still, as silent as statues, but as I sank onto the bench, they began to move quietly, getting dressed. No one talked to me. I supposed they all thought Jane was right. My hands were trembling. I had to clench them into fists to make them stop. Most of the other girls dressed quickly, and soon I was alone. I slowly pulled my clothes on. My body felt like it was a hundred years old — slow and creaky and drained of energy. I picked up my gym clothes and my basketball uniform and put them in my locker, then I walked upstairs, got my coat and my homework and trudged outside to the bus stop. The school buses were gone for the day — I had to wait for the city bus.

The wind was ice cold, and grey November clouds scudded across the sky. I pulled up the collar of my coat, reached inside my backpack for a bus ticket — Dad had bought me a book of them for emergencies — and sat down inside the glass shelter.

The hard knot of anger in my stomach began to dissolve. I knew I'd been ... well, not exactly nice to other kids sometimes. I hate being laughed at. There was this kid in elementary school who used to bug me at recess all the time. He used to call me "Kallana, Kallana, nose like a banana" in front of everybody, or he would yell, "Here comes Ugly!" and run. I know it sounds stupid, but when you're only seven years old, dumb names like that really hurt. So after half a year of this, I started insulting him back, really razoring him, and he shut up. The problem was, those horrible nicknames had caught on, all because of him. So I got good at thinking up insults for any kid who used them or laughed at me. Then it sort of became a habit. I just did it without thinking about it, whether someone deserved it or not.

Last year, I bugged Jane a lot about looking like a boy because she dressed in her brother's clothes. I joked about her still being as flat as a board, even though I could see she was dying of embarrassment. I winced at the memory. It was stupid, and I don't really know why I said it. But what's the big deal? I don't have much of a chest yet, either. And anyway, that's no reason to call me a liar.

Maybe Jane really did hate me. That gave me a queer feeling in my stomach. I never wanted anyone to hate me.

The bus pulled up, and I got on. All the long way home, I stared out the window, thinking about everything that had happened at the game. This was the worst day of my life, I decided. And I could tell you one thing: I wasn't ever going to set foot on a basketball court again.

I got off at the bus-stop near my house and walked home with my head up. I wouldn't cry. No matter how awful this afternoon had been, I wouldn't cry. My mother was home, but she was on the phone, so it was easy for me to wave quickly at her and rush up the stairs to my room.

I threw down my backpack and flopped face down on the bed. I buried my face in the stuffed animals surrounding my pillow, picked up my favourite one — a soft, plush purple giraffe — and clutched him to my chest.

"I had a horrible day, Wilson," I told him. "The absolute worst. If the whole world doesn't hate me, then they think I'm a total geek." And I wasn't sure which was worse. I'd tried so hard to be the person in control. I wasn't supposed to be a geek.

"Well, it won't happen again," I said, feeling my face turn hot at just the memory of the game. "Not ever." I held Wilson tighter.

"Kall?" My dad tapped lightly on the door. "I *thought* I heard you come in."

I braced myself for what I knew was coming. "Hi, Dad, I didn't know you were home."

"How was the game?"

"Awful."

Dad looked surprised. "Really? Why?" He pulled my desk chair over next to the bed and sat down.

"I flubbed up royally. Big time."

"How?"

"Where should I start the list?" I said, suddenly angry at him. After all, it was *his* fault that I'd had to play basketball in the first place. I sat up abruptly and began ticking off the facts on my fingers. "I didn't know the rules, so I had no idea what I was doing. I threw the ball into the court after the other team scored, but I didn't know I was supposed to pass it to one of our players, so the other team got it and scored again. I couldn't cover the girl I was supposed to on the other team, so she racked up a million points. I jammed out when I was supposed to do a free throw and walked off the court. I told the coach I was sick, but the truth was, I was too scared to do it. Then to finish this brilliant day, I accidently locked another girl's gym shoes in my locker, and I didn't know, so when she couldn't find them, the coach benched her for the game. She was completely ticked off about that, and afterwards when we were all getting dressed, her shoes fell out of my locker, so she thinks I did it on purpose to keep her from playing."

"Hmmm."

"I suck at basketball. I hate it."

Dad just looked at me with a contemplative eye.

"I'm never playing it again. I mean it."

"Kallie, you've only played one game."

"I don't care."

"You haven't even given it a chance."

"I don't need to. I can tell already that I hate it."

"You need to play more than one game to get good at a sport. You can't expect to just walk out there and be a super-star."

"I don't want to be a superstar. I just don't want to play basketball. I never did. You wanted me to."

"And I still want you to."

"Well, forget it."

"No."

"Dad! I mean it." I frowned at him.

"So do I." Dad leaned forward. "Kallana, this is more important than feeling embarrassed because you made a few mistakes today. Playing on a team teaches you things that you can't get anyplace else. It teaches you how to work with other people, and it gives you self-confidence. I don't think you should lose that, just because you feel silly about not knowing how to play. Besides, don't be so hard on yourself — everybody knows you're a beginner. The coach didn't expect you to be an expert."

I rolled my eyes. This was so parental. The trouble was, Dad didn't have a clue. Kids *don't* give you a break if you're a beginner. They *do* laugh if you mess up. Either Dad was never a kid, or he'd completely forgotten what it was like to be one.

"It doesn't matter, Dad. I'm quitting the team."

"Kallana, you've already told the coach you'd join. What about your sense of commitment? Your sense of school spirit?"

"They walked out the door about an hour ago, along with my sense of humour."

"Don't get smart with me, young lady."

I gave a loud sigh, so he would get the idea that I was losing patience. "Dad, I'm not doing it."

"Kall, I didn't want to play the heavy here, but I am the parent, and you are the child. I am not asking you. I am telling you. You are not quitting the team. You haven't given me one valid reason why you should."

"I have so! That is so unfair!" I sat up and clenched my fists. "You can't do this to me!"

"Playing one game isn't enough for you to make this decision. If you still feel like you want to quit after five games, I'll consider it. But only if it means you won't be letting the team down in any major way."

"Believe me, my leaving would be a definite improvement."

"Ms. Wright obviously didn't think so, or she wouldn't have asked you to join in the first place."

I stayed silent for a minute. "Dad, you don't understand. I can't go back. It was horrible."

"You *can* go back. It'll build character." Dad grinned and stood up, and I knew there was nothing more I could say. I was going to have to go back on that basketball court. When Dad left the room, I picked up Wilson, and the tears I'd been holding back all afternoon ran down my cheeks, making damp splotches in his soft fur.

7

Jane and I

I survived another session of practice. Jane wouldn't speak to me, and I just barely managed to follow what Ms. Wright told me to do. But I dreaded the next game, and the following Wednesday started badly. I woke up to my mother's voice, clipped and stiff, like rocks falling on ice. I couldn't make out the words, but when I poked my head into the hallway, she stopped, and Dad managed a weak grin. "Hey, Kallie. I'm off for a few days. Give your old Dad a hug."

I didn't especially want to. I'd been avoiding him since his big 'I'm-the-parent' discussion, but I gave him a quick squeeze. "Where are you going?"

"North. Near Cold Lake. I got an assignment from an ad firm to do photos for an advertising campaign."

"For what? Igloos?"

Dad smiled. "Hiking clothes. Jackets, boots. That sort of thing."

"Oh. Good. Does it pay lots?"

Dad's smile faded. "Some. It's not bad."

Mom stayed silent. I could tell she wanted to say something, but she held it back. I waited, uncertain, then said, "I guess I'd better get ready for school."

"Guess you'd better. See you in a few days, Kall. I'm driving up, so I'm off now."

"Okay." I watched while Dad hurried down the stairs. Mom gave a short sigh.

"I'll get some breakfast for you," she said. "Hurry, or you'll be late."

Surprised, I just nodded. Usually I made my own breakfast, or if I was really late, skipped it completely. In my room, I pulled on some clothes, for once not really caring enough to be creative. Jeans and a maroon cardigan with a matching top underneath was good enough. I did up the top button on the cardigan, leaving the rest unbuttoned, and slid my feet into my navy platform runners. Still cool. Not too fancy, but still cool.

Mom had defrosted some bakery blueberry muffins from the freezer. So much for a gourmet breakfast. Still, it was more than I'd learned to expect. Mom usually cooked one meal a day — supper — and we were left to fend for ourselves for the rest. And often supper was a frozen dinner because Mom had a late meeting, or needed to finish up some work.

I bit into a muffin and watched while my mother poured herself some coffee and sat down. She didn't seem angry, but there was something going on. I could feel it.

"How's school going?" she asked.

"Fine," I answered.

"Everything okay?"

"I guess so."

"How about this basketball team your father pushed you into?"

So that was it. For some reason I felt defensive. I could have easily told the truth — Mom probably would have told me I could quit, and the heck with what Dad said. But something kept me from saying it. I didn't want her to blame Dad for what had happened. "It's okay," I said.

"No problems?"

"None." I nearly choked on the word. "I'd better go, Mom. I'll miss the bus." I picked up the last half of muffin and ran upstairs to collect my homework, which I hadn't done, and my jacket. Then I raced for the bus-stop. The bus pulled up just as I reached the stop, and I climbed on.

At school, Taylor Anne and Chelsea met me by the front door, and immediately began giggling.

"Guess what we heard," Taylor Anne said.

"What?"

"Kyle Javer asked Amy to go out with him. Like on a *date*."

"Really? That's cool." This news would have been absorbing at any other time, but for some reason, I couldn't get interested. I only half-listened while Chelsea shrieked and Taylor giggled. I kept wondering what I would do at basketball practice that afternoon. How would I face Jane again?

"So, Kall. You want to go to the mall with me and Tay after school?" Chelsea asked. "We're going to try on nail polish at the drugstore."

"After school? Um ... I can't."

"Why not? You haven't hung out with us since last week. What's the matter?"

"Nothing. I just have some ... stuff to do."

"What kind of stuff?"

Oh, geez. What could I say? I didn't want them to know about the basketball team, not yet. I just couldn't put up with any more teasing. "I have a dentist appointment," I lied.

"Oh. Too bad. How about tomorrow?"

"Maybe." I wasn't sure if we had practice tomorrow.

The bell rang and we hurried to class. Through the whole day, the thought of basketball practice loomed large and menacing, because I dreaded it so much. I was terrified the coach would tell us we had another game tomorrow — someone had mentioned that most games were on Thursdays. By the time dismissal rolled around, my knees felt boneless, hardly able to support my weight, and I couldn't keep my fingers from drumming endlessly on whatever surface was handy.

I managed to get to the gym. I exhaled slowly and stood straight up. Whatever else happened, Jane would never, ever know I was afraid — afraid to face her, afraid to put a basketball in my hands again, afraid to make a fool of myself.

Ms. Wright was waiting. She gave me a cheerful smile, her brown eyes merry. "How are you feeling today, Kallana?"

"All right," I said. Ms. Wright had been asking me that since the game, but something about her concern made me feel warm inside.

"Ready to try some passing drills in a practice game today?"

"I guess so."

"Good girl. We'll work on some defence, too. I have some tips that'll help you. But you handled Daria pretty well last week, considering it was your first game." The praise was like salve, even if Ms. Wright was only being nice. Some of the hurt places inside me began to smooth away.

"Really?"

"Absolutely. I taught at Daria's school before I came to Meadowpark this year. She's played every sport I can think of, and basketball is her favourite. You did well, keeping up with her."

"Thanks." I thought about that. Then I took a deep breath. "Do we have a game tomorrow?"

Ms. Wright looked surprised. "No. Didn't I tell you? Last week's game was just an exhibition. Our next game is in two weeks." She laughed at the look of relief that must have been obvious on my face. "Gets you off the hook for a while longer, eh Kallana?" She tapped my shoulder. "Don't worry. You'll have everything under control by then."

I hoped so.

"Better go get into your practice clothes. We don't want to waste any time, today." Ms. Wright opened one of the storage rooms and began to bring out the tall buckets full of basketballs.

I went down to the locker-room. The other girls were already there, and they all fell silent when I walked in. I braced myself, but Jane turned her back and began putting new shoelaces into her runners. The rest of the girls waited to see what would happen, but I just undid my locker and pulled on a pair of shorts and a T-shirt. Then I walked over to the mirror and put a barrette in the front of my hair to keep it out of my eyes and went back to the gym. No one had said a word to me.

Ms. Wright clapped her hands for attention. "All right, ladies. Let's begin with a warm-up. Do some stretches on the floor, then we'll run a few laps. You have to be in good cardiovascular shape to play hard for a whole game, even when we sub out. You'll be surprised how tired you feel." She led us through some leg and arms stretches, then ran with us around the gym for ten laps.

I was breathing hard when we were done. I tried not to notice how Jane and a few others hardly even looked tired.

The coach divided us into two teams. Jane was on the opposite side, and Ms. Wright started the game, telling us to use passing skills whenever possible. I didn't really know what I was doing, and I had no idea who I was supposed to cover, but Jane stepped in front me every chance she got, so I decided that I would check her. She began dodging me, dribbling the ball, almost taunting me to come and get it. As soon as I lunged for it, she would throw it to one of her players.

After a few minutes of this, I began to get ticked off. I started covering her more closely, with my arms stretched out, trying to prevent her from passing the ball. Jane whirled around, trying to get away, but I stuck to her like glue. When she finally tried to toss the ball over my head to a team-mate, I leaped and knocked it down. It bounced on the gym floor, and Marty, who was on my team, scooped it up and, dribbling fast, ran for the basket.

"Great defence, Kallana!" Ms. Wright shouted. "Way to cover her!" She looked delighted. I felt a surge of confidence. But Jane scowled, her mouth set in angry ridges.

The next time Jane had the ball, she jostled past me, shoving me out of the way. I scrambled after her, and she pushed past again. She threw the ball toward the hoop, watched it swish through the basket, then gave me a triumphant look. She still hadn't said one word to me, but she was clearly thinking, "Top that!"

Ms. Wright gave the ball to Marty to toss back into play. She flipped it to me, then dashed back on the court. I began to bounce the ball, running with it, then passed it back to Marty. She raced for the opposite basket, and I followed, with Jane doing her best to cut in front me. I let her, then dodged to the side, but I wasn't completely prepared when Marty passed the ball back to me. Jane looked back and dived toward me. My stomach clenched, and I did the only thing I could think of — I jumped and threw the ball toward the basket. I knew before it hit the rim that it wouldn't make it in. I ran for the rebound. So did Jane.

The ball bounced off the rim. I leaped for it, and so did Jane. We collided hard in mid-air, and I fell with a thump on the gym floor. The breath went out of me with a whoosh, but in a second I was on my feet, blazing with rage.

"You did that on purpose!" I hissed.

Jane narrowed her eyes. "I didn't, but I wish I had."

"I didn't take your stupid sneakers, so get over it, okay?"

"Like I'd believe *you*." Jane crossed her arms. "Not in this lifetime."

"Whatever." I used my best you're-an-idiot tone of voice. "Just try to save the body-checking for hockey, okay?"

"What's the matter, Kallana? Can't take a little bump on the court? Maybe you should stick to your little fashion friends."

"Maybe you should stick to playing with boys," I snapped, "since you look so much like one."

Jane flushed red as my eyes swept over her cropped brown hair, square jaw, and boyishly thin body. Jane knew she wasn't pretty. Neither was I, so I knew how to drive that point home to her.

Jane grabbed the basketball and threw it at me with all her strength. My hands automatically reached out to catch it, and the force of it made me step backwards. "I don't have to be a fashion queen to play basketball," she said angrily.

"That's for sure," I answered, my voice laced with sarcasm.

"Why don't you just shut up?" Jane shouted.

"Make me!" I yelled back.

"Girls, settle down. That's enough." Ms. Wright stepped on the court. She'd only heard the last bit, since Jane and I had been practically whispering until the end. "It was an accident. These things happen on the court." She checked her watch. "We're almost out of time, anyway. Stretch out a bit, and we'll call it a day. I'll see you all at practice tomorrow. The first game of the regular season is in two weeks — so I want us to concentrate on fundamentals and really sharp teamwork until then." She walked down to the end of the gym and began picking up stray basketballs and putting them in the bins.

Marty led the other girls in some half-hearted stretches, but I sank onto the nearest bleacher, my stomach still knotted with anger. Jane turned and stalked out of the gym, her shoulders and back as rigid as an army sergeant's.

8

Home Sweet Home

I heard the yelling before I even opened the front door. I paused with my hand on the knob, not wanting to go in. It seemed like my whole day had been fighting. I could hear Dad's voice.

"I can't help it that they cancelled the assignment. And it's not like I won't get it again, when the weather clears up north."

"That's not the point. The point is, we can never depend on your pay cheque. And when money does come in, you spend it the minute you cash the cheque! I can't do everything, Greg. I'm the one who pays the bills. I'm the one who does the housework and makes the meals —"

"And fine ones they are, too," Dad said sarcastically.

The sarcasm enraged my mother. "Don't you patronize me! If I have to serve frozen dinners three nights out of four, it's because you never lift a finger around here to help me! I'm running a business, Greg. I am not a housewife. I do not have time to be everything to everybody!" She was yelling so loud, I could practically hear the windows rattle.

"No. Of course not. You especially don't have time to be a mother to your daughter." Now Dad sounded angry, too.

"I'm here when Kallana comes home from school, and I'm here before she leaves in the morning. That's more than most kids with working mothers get."

"Lydia, you are more dense than I give you credit for. That girl is practically begging for your attention, and you don't even see it. Just because you're here in the same house with her, doesn't mean she's getting what she needs. She's obsessed with those ridiculous clothes and she diets — *diets!* — just so she can fit into them. She's not even thirteen yet! You can't tell me that that's not a direct result of your modelling business —"

I turned the doorknob, and both my parents swivelled in surprise.

"Kallie!" Dad dredged up a smile for me.

"Hi, Dad." I was quiet. "How come you're home?"

My mother shot him a ferocious look.

"I started out this morning, but I got a call on my cell phone to turn back. Apparently Cold Lake is having a sudden snowstorm that'll last for a few days. So we're going to try to reschedule for next week."

"Oh."

Dad shifted uncomfortably. "Want to go out for dinner, Kall? We could go to The Golden Dragon for Chinese in about an hour or so."

Mom made a strangled sound. "With what money?"

Dad gave her a look.

I glanced from one to the other. "Uh … sure. I guess I'll go do my homework, then." I turned and bolted up the stairs, then I opened and closed the door to my room without going in, and knelt on the landing. I could still hear everything.

"That's just exactly what I mean. A fifty-dollar dinner is an expense we don't need right now. But you don't even think twice!"

"Lyd, would you quit counting pennies and live a little, for a change?"

I could hear the clenched, tight tone in my mother's voice. "Someone around here has to be responsible."

"I wouldn't say that description exactly fits you, the way you ignore your daughter."

"I don't ignore her. But I'm getting tired of catering to Kallana's every need. I've done it since she was a baby, and I'm more than tired of catering to yours. I'm not a single parent here, you know. You've been too wrapped up in your own affairs to notice when I needed your help, and Kallana is a big girl now. She doesn't need her mother hovering over her every minute of the day."

"Don't make it sound like you're some martyred mother. You never hovered over Kallana, even in your best moments."

There was a little pause, then my mother spoke. Her voice was low, but full of fury. "This conversation is over." I heard the click of her shoes on the tiles, then the front door slammed.

I swallowed hard and crept into my room. My parents had argued before. Lots of times. But something about this argument made my stomach knot up again, this time with fear. They'd had too many arguments like this lately. The words were different each time, but somehow the same. And there was never a happy ending to these arguments, the way there used to be.

Dinner time rolled around, and Mom still hadn't come back.

"Want to go out? We can bring something back for Mom." Dad spoke easily, as if everything was all right.

"Um, no. I guess not. I'm not that hungry. Maybe I'll just make a sandwich or something."

"A sandwich? Is this the same girl who polished off two bowls of hot-and-sour soup and *eight* spring rolls the last time we went to The Golden Dragon?" Dad peered at me closely. "No, I don't think it is. Clever disguise, whoever you are. You nearly had me fooled. What have you done with the real Kallana Ohlmstead?"

I forced a laugh. Dad's clowning always made me giggle when I was little, but this time I knew he was just putting on a show for my benefit, and inside I was more worried than ever. Where was Mom?

Dad saw through me. "Come on, Kallie. Don't let Mom's comments get you down. We can afford to go out and grab some supper. It won't put us in the poorhouse."

"But why was she saying those things, then?"

"Because we're in a bit over our heads with the mortgage on the house, and I get paid here and there for my photos, so she worries when we can't count on money coming in. But it'll be all right."

I wanted to say, "Promise?" But I didn't. I knew in my heart my dad couldn't promise me that, and I didn't want him to lie to me. So I kept silent, got my jacket, and let him take me out for dinner, even though every mouthful of spring roll nearly choked me.

"If we don't have enough money to pay for the house, how come Mom gives me so much for clothes and things?" I asked in the parking lot afterwards.

Dad frowned. "Because she feels guilty, so when she has it, throwing money at you is one way to make herself feel better. But we have enough, Kall. Just not as much as your mother wants."

When we got home, Mom was waiting. She didn't look angry any more. But she did have an immovable expression on her face, and she waited calmly until I'd gone upstairs. Then I heard my parents' voices, low and flat, from the family room. I couldn't tell what they were saying, but I heard them talking long into the night.

9

A Rotten Day

Worry and irritation had turned my stomach into a mass of knots. Something was definitely up at home. Mom and Dad weren't saying much, to me or to each other, but I could feel the tension. Strange as it was, my only relief was basketball practice, even if Jane was doing her best to make me feel like a loser. It was the only thing that demanded my total concentration, and all that racing around and throwing balls relieved some of the anger and fear that churned inside me.

Tuesday afternoon at school, I wasn't thinking about Mom or Dad. I had just tossed my books in my locker after the dismissal bell and grabbed my gym shoes, when I heard a familiar voice.

"Kallie?" Dad was walking down the hall. Mom was behind him, still dressed for work. I froze.

"What are you doing here?" I asked, acutely aware of the curious stares from other students. Parents don't usually show up in school hallways without a reason.

Dad looked uncomfortable. "We wanted to pick you up, today, instead of having you take the bus."

"But I have basketball," I said, my voice higher pitched than usual. Dad glanced at Mom.

"You can miss it today," Mom said.

"But the season starts in a week — we have a game next Thursday," I said. I looked at Dad helplessly.

Dad shook his head. "It'll be all right. Come on, Kallie."

And then I knew. *I knew.* And I didn't want to hear it. But I swallowed and played along. I grabbed some books — I didn't even bother to see if they were the right ones for homework — and my jacket and followed them outside.

"Where are we going?" I asked once we were in the car.

"We thought maybe we'd go someplace fun — the planetarium, a matinée movie, whatever you want. Then out for dinner. You choose," Dad said.

Why? I thought bitterly. So we can celebrate our last day as a family? "No, thanks," I said. "I'd rather go home."

Dad turned in his seat, and I gave him a steady stare. He nodded and looked at Mom. "Home it is."

Mom started to speak, then changed her mind. We rode home in silence.

When we got inside the house, I took off my jacket, tossed my books on the floor, and headed straight for my room. Then I lay on my bed and waited, pretending to read a book. The minutes clicked by on my alarm clock. Exactly twelve minutes later, I heard them coming up the stairs. A tight, frightened feeling rose inside me. *I don't want to hear it. I don't want to hear it.*

There was a gentle knock on my bedroom door. I glanced up as both Mom and Dad came into the room.

"Kallie, we need to talk to you." Dad sat beside me on the edge of the bed. I sat up and wiggled backwards until my back was against the headboard. My stomach clenched.

"Dad, I'm not feeling too great. Can we talk about this later?" I said desperately.

"Kall," Dad said gently. I lowered my eyes.

Mom got straight to the point. "Dad and I have decided to separate."

I looked at them, and my voice choked. "You're getting a divorce?" I could barely get the words out.

"No," Dad said. "We're going to try a trial separation. Mom's moving out for a while."

"*Mom's* moving out?" I stared at her, but she avoided my gaze. I felt a wave of despair come crashing down on me. Mothers weren't supposed to abandon their children. Was I so awful that she couldn't stand me any more? I'd tried so hard to be the kind of girl she liked — pretty, trendy, in control. Why couldn't she love me the way I wanted her to?

"We need some time to sort things out, Kallie," Dad said. "Don't worry. Everything will work out."

"No, it won't!" I yelled. I sat up straight and glared, first at my dad, then at my mother. "Nothing will ever be all right again!" All the rage and frustration I'd felt at basketball in the past weeks, and the overwhelming sadness I felt now, I couldn't control for one second longer. "Get out! Both of you, just get out!"

Dad and Mom looked at each other and quickly left the room. I grabbed Wilson, the purple giraffe, and pitched him at the closing door as hard as I could. I hated my parents. I hated Jane. I hated the whole world. And I hated myself.

I buried my face in my pillow and sobbed.

* * *

At basketball practice the next afternoon, I raced to the centre of the court and fired the ball toward the rim with every ounce of strength I had.

"A little too hard, Kallana," Ms. Wright called. "Remember, accuracy is better than strength. You don't have to try for a three-pointer."

By now I'd learned that if you sank a basket from behind a line near the middle of the court, it was worth three points, instead of two. But I hadn't been concentrating on the basket, I'd been trying to throw away the rage and hurt I felt. How could my parents do this to me? How could my mother do this?

The quick pounding of the basketball against the gym floor matched the thudding of my heart against my ribs. Sweat trickled down my face, and my breath came fast and hard. I chased Marty, who was my practice opponent, but she neatly evaded me, her brown braid whipping out behind her as she twisted away and raced down the court. I panted after her, but Marty was fast. Her thin legs and spidery arms moved in a blur. She went for a pass, but I slowed to a stop, my breath catching painfully in my side.

Jane jostled me from behind, and I felt a surge of anger. Side cramp forgotten, I turned on her like a tiger. She had the ball now, and before she knew what had happened, I whipped it out from under her hand and was flying down the court. I did a lay-up and popped the ball neatly into the basket. Jane stared at me with her mouth open.

"All right, Kallana!" Ms. Wright clapped her hands. "Those are the moves I want to see!"

Jane was a little more cautious whenever she guarded me for the rest of the practice game, and I smiled to myself. Marty covered me when Jane did not, and she was pleased when I broke away from her to send a pass to one of my team-mates.

"You're really okay, Kallana," Marty said, slapping me a high-five. "Make sure you do that in Thursday's game, okay?"

"Sure."

By the time practice was over, I'd worked harder than I ever had in my life. My legs trembled with fatigue, and sweat was running down my temples. But I felt better, somehow, as if some of the awful feelings that lingered inside of me had run out and washed away.

Hard to believe of me, who was always so careful about how I looked. I knew I'd never looked worse. My hair was sticky with sweat and frizzled in all directions. My shorts and jersey drooped with dampness, and my face felt so hot, I was sure it was as red as a beet. But I hardly cared, until I followed Jane and Marty out of the gym and saw Taylor Anne and Chelsea leaning up against the hallway wall, chatting up a couple of guys from the ninth grade basketball team. I could tell who they were because the boys wore jerseys like mine, except they weren't all gross and sweaty, and their muscles showed.

Taylor Anne saw me first. Her jaw dropped in shock, and she joggled Chelsea with her elbow, her eyes never leaving my face.

Chelsea's reaction was even funnier. She stopped in mid-sentence, and while the guys looked at her expectantly, she completely forgot what she was going to say.

I hurried down the stairs to the locker-room and ducked inside. I changed as fast as I could and whipped a brush through my hair. Not that it helped much. When I looked in the mirror, I still looked red and sweaty, and my hair was damp at the temples, but fuzzy and stiff lower down. I sighed impatiently and pulled my black wool tam — thank goodness I'd left it in my locker — down as low over my ears as it would go. Then I hurried out of the room.

But even though I sneaked up the backstairs, Taylor and Chelsea were waiting, and they pounced on me as I went past the gym.

"Kall, what the heck are you doing? Are you on the basketball team? You said you wouldn't play!" They peppered me with questions.

"Dad's making me," I said. This was the last thing I felt like talking about. And yet, I couldn't even imagine telling them about my mom and dad. So what *would* I talk to them about?

"But you never told us! How come? How long have you been playing? Is that why you haven't been hanging our with us after school?" Chelsea asked.

"Yeah. And I've been playing for about two weeks."

"*Two weeks!*"

"Uh, huh."

"So … is it fun?" Taylor Anne asked.

"Sometimes. Today was okay. But mostly not really."

Chelsea began to laugh. "I can't believe you're wearing one of those awful uniforms. You should have seen yourself when you came out of the gym earlier. I thought I'd die!"

I felt my cheeks turn red.

"Kallana the athlete. I don't think I can stand it!" Chelsea leaned against Taylor and giggled harder. "I mean, basketball is so butchy. Why didn't you pick a sport where you don't have to sweat so much?"

Jane suddenly appeared from behind me, and it was obvious from her expression that she'd heard what Chelsea had said.

"I hate to tell you this, Chelsea, but filing your nails hasn't become an official sport yet," Jane said.

Chelsea stopped laughing. "I don't think we were talking to you," she said rudely.

"The whole world could hear you. If you want a private conversation, go in the bathroom like everyone else." Jane turned and walked away.

"Eeeeew! How can you stand having to play with her on the team?" Chelsea said.

"She's not so bad," I said. Whether I believed that or not didn't matter. I couldn't let Chelsea feel sorry for me for any reason. Besides, I did feel glad that Jane had shut Chelsea up.

"C'mon, let's walk to the bus-stop. Who were those guys you were talking to?"

While I listened to Chelsea's enthusiastic reply, in the back of my mind I kept remembering how I had felt when I walked out of the gym. I hadn't cared at all how I looked, and it felt good. Then seeing Taylor and Chelsea brought my whole world crashing back down. I remembered that I was Kallana, the queen of cool. I remembered that I wasn't pretty, and that I had to hide that fact behind trendy clothes. I remembered that my mother wouldn't use me as a model if her life depended on it. And as much as I tried to push the thought away, I remembered that she was leaving me and my dad.

All the good feelings that had happened during basketball practice evaporated, and I was left feeling hollow and empty again. It was a very long walk to the bus-stop.

10

Back in Control

When I dressed for school the next day, I paid special attention to how I looked. I'd showered the night before and shampooed my hair, so I took a spray bottle and dampened it before I blow-dried with a round brush, the way one of my magazines instructed. It didn't turn out exactly like the picture, but it was close enough. I parted my hair on the side, and sleeked the thicker half across my forehead and pinned it with some miniature butterfly clips by my temple. Then I borrowed some powder blush and mascara from my mother's bathroom and carefully dabbed it on. I'd seen her do it enough times to copy it, but I still made a mess on one eyelid and had to wipe it off with tissue. I had my own lip gloss — frosty pale pink. I spread it over my lips and blotted it with another tissue, so it wouldn't look heavy.

Mom didn't want me to wear much makeup yet, but I doubted that she'd be able to tell I had it on, unless she looked closely. The mascara was thinly applied, darkening only the tips of my eyelashes, and the blush was light, making me look just a little less pale. The lip gloss was okay. I'm allowed to wear that.

Now for the clothes. I stood pondering the contents of my closet before I settled on a short, charcoal grey skirt made of soft wool and a matching grey short sleeved sweater with steel buttons down the front. I did up the top three buttons and took the rest off with a pair of manicure scissors, so the sweater sloped back over my stomach, showing my belly button. I decided my black tights looked weird, so I put on black ankle socks and my mary janes with the chunky heels, leaving my legs bare. It was a bit cold outside, but I figured I could put up with it. The result at school would be worth it. This look was too sophisticated for me to worry about being cold. I finished up with my charm necklace. It was a jade dolphin strung on thick black string, and it was just tight enough that the dolphin rested in the hollow of my throat.

There. Perfect. I admired myself in the mirror. I looked casual, but trendy and very, very cool. I grabbed a thick cranberry-coloured blazer that I'd once borrowed from my mother and forgotten to return and dashed out of the house. I didn't want either of my parents to see me, because they'd definitely make me change. Even my mother, who couldn't care less what I did, wouldn't let me out of the house in late November with legs bare-skinned to the thigh.

Once I'd stopped running a half block from the house, I began to realize that I'd made a major mistake. The wind was like a blast from the North Pole. It was snowing, but not with loose, fleecy flakes. These snowflakes were like diamonds chips — hard and glittering under the dimming glow of the streetlamps — and they stung the backs of my legs with each gust of wind.

It was too late to turn back — I'd miss the bus. I ran the rest of the way to the bus-stop. Once I was there, I shifted my legs close to each other and wrapped my arms around myself, but within three seconds the entire lower half of my body was numb and purple with cold. My breath made icy clouds in the air, and I danced discreetly on the sidewalk, trying to keep warm.

When the bus finally pulled up, I could hardly make my legs move. I stumbled up the steps of the bus and saw the driver shake her head at me. "Crazy kid," I heard her mumble. "Fourteen degrees below zero, and she's wearing shorts."

"Skirt," I corrected through frozen lips. I dropped into the nearest seat, and the warmth from the vinyl was like heaven on my bare flesh.

When the bus pulled up next to the school, a new purgatory awaited me. It's a school rule that unless it's cold enough for frostbite, the students must remain outside the school until the first bell rings. I was fifteen minutes early, and waiting with that hypothermic wind whistling around my legs was enough to make me swear through chattering teeth never to dress in the name of fashion again. Looking good wasn't worth this kind of effort.

But once the bell rang and I was inside, my skin began to thaw, and I felt a little better. I really did look like the girls in the magazines. Most of the other girls at school were wearing jeans with unimaginative sweaters and sweatshirts. When I hung up my blazer in my locker and straightened my skirt, I felt that old satisfaction well up in me. I might not be beautiful, but at least I could be cool.

When I went to class, Mrs. Kilton eyed me, and I felt a chill run through me. I'd forgotten about her. She didn't say anything at first, and when she had called the roll, I felt reasonably safe. But then she asked me to come up to her desk, and instead of speaking to me there in front of the class, she led me into the hall.

Only a few students were still hurrying to homeroom — the hall was almost empty. Mrs. Kilton's voice was quiet but firm.

"Kallana, do you remember the note I sent home with you on the first day of school?"

I nodded.

"Did your mother let you read it?"

I nodded again. She hadn't, but it didn't matter. I knew what the note had said.

"I don't want to embarrass you, Kallana, but what you are wearing is not appropriate. You'll have to change into something else."

"But I have nothing else to wear!" I wailed. I'd taken my basketball uniform and gym gear home to be washed the night before, but I'd forgotten to put them in the dryer. They were hanging in my locker now — I hoped they'd be dry by practice — and anyway, if Mrs. Kilton considered a skirt to be inappropriate, she would hardly allow gym shorts.

"I'm going to have to send you home, then, to get some other clothes."

"No!" I said, aghast at the prospect of facing that wind again. "You can't! Is this legal? Isn't there some law about freedom of choice?"

Mrs. Kilton's expression turned grim. "Be that as it may, a school is no place for clothing that barely covers the essentials. Besides, this is hardly the kind of weather for an outfit like that. I'm sorry, Kallana."

I turned away, but not before a hiccuping sob escaped from my throat. I couldn't help it. I felt like all I'd done in the last few days was cry, but it was no use. I kept trying so hard to be special, and no matter what I did, someone didn't like it.

Mrs. Kilton made futile gestures toward me, but I kept stepping back. If Ms. Wright hadn't happened to come down the hall at that moment, I don't know what I would have done.

"Kallana! What's the matter?" she said, with a concerned look on her face.

I couldn't answer. I was crying too hard.

Mrs. Kilton explained. "Kallana's been asked before not to wear clothing that is ... well, not appropriate for school. I've asked her to go home for some extra clothes."

Ms. Wright put her arm around my shoulder and gave me a squeeze. "Kallana, it's all right. Stop crying now." She looked at Mrs. Kilton. "All right if I borrow her for a while?"

Mrs. Kilton nodded, and she waited until we were part way down the hall before disappearing back into the classroom. Ms. Wright led me to her tiny, cramped office next to the gym. She tossed an old sweatshirt and a stack of paper off the one extra chair and let me sit down. She pulled the desk chair out from its place and sat down across from me.

"Want to talk?" she asked.

I glanced at the open door, afraid someone might overhear me. Ms. Wright understood, and shut it with her foot. "Okay now?"

I nodded, then I tried to explain. I told her about how dressing up made me feel, and how I had practically frozen solid at the bus-stop that morning and couldn't face doing that again now that Mrs. Kilton had told me I'd have to go home. I told her how great I had felt after basketball practice, until my friends had shown up. I told her all about feeling ugly, and why that was the reason my mother didn't love me. And then I told her about Mom leaving. I'd been crying the whole time, and now the words were running together until I could hardly tell what I was saying. But Ms. Wright only nodded and handed me tissues, making remarks here and there that let me know she understood.

After I finally wound down, Ms. Wright straightened up. "All right. Let's deal with one problem at a time, here. I have some clean sweatpants and a few clean gym shirts you could wear today. It won't be very fashionable, but at least you won't have to go home."

"Okay." By this point, I didn't care what I wore.

"Next problem. Kallana, you may not feel attractive right now, but believe me when I say that most girls your age don't. Even the pretty ones. I've raised two daughters myself and

I've taught junior high for twelve years, and I know. Do you remember your first game, and the girl who played opposite you?"

"Daria?"

"Yes. I taught Daria last year, like I told you. Daria doesn't think she's pretty, either. She told me once that she thought her brother's hamster was prettier than she was."

"Really?" I thought about that. It seemed weird that someone as beautiful as Daria could feel ugly, too.

"So what I'm trying to say, Kallana, is that no matter how physically attractive a person is, if they don't see that beauty when they look in the mirror, then what others see doesn't matter." Ms. Wright leaned forward earnestly. "You have to feel comfortable with yourself. Do you understand?"

"I guess so. But I really *am* disgustingly ugly. I'm not like Daria. And wearing cool clothes at least makes me feel kind of … you know …." I floundered, unable to explain what I meant. "Cool," I finished lamely.

But Ms. Wright nodded, like she understood. "I know. But you can still feel 'cool' and not wear things that will make Mrs. Kilton send you home, can't you?"

"I guess so." I shrugged.

"Besides, from what you've been telling me, you're just hiding behind these clothes, anyway. You said you felt great after practice yesterday, before you bumped into your friends. Any idea why?"

I shook my head.

"I'm guessing it's because you achieved something that had nothing at all to do with how pretty you are."

I smiled. She was right.

The intercom buzzed on Ms. Wright's desk. The school secretary's voice reminded Ms. Wright there was a meeting in five minutes.

"Thank you. I'll be there in a moment." Ms. Wright clicked the intercom button off.

I stood up.

"Kallana, for the record, I don't think you're disgustingly ugly. And what's more, I think you're a pretty nice kid." Ms. Wright smiled at me, and I felt my heart swell inside my chest. But I didn't know how to say thank you, to tell her how much those words meant to me. So instead, I managed a smile and reached for the doorknob.

11

A Meeting with Mom

The apartment looked like a classy hotel room. From where I stood in the front entrance, I could see a big dried floral arrangement in a brass pot on the glass-and-wrought-iron coffee table. The beige walls were hung with abstract water-colour prints, painted mostly in dark reds, navy blue and greens, which matched the deep-seated sofa and armchairs. The eating nook held a small oak table with four chairs, and the tiny kitchen was brilliant white, with dark green counter tops.

I'd been here before. This was the apartment Mom sub-leased for her business. She used it for clients and models from other cities when they came to Calgary for business purposes. Some of the models Mom managed ended up going to Toronto or New York, but there were a few from smaller cities or towns that came in for local work. When that happened, Mom let them stay here.

My mother really does more than just find models. I'd never thought about it much, but she started a marketing end of the company as well, so advertising clients could come to her and get a kind of one-stop shopping thing. Some of the companies are even brand names I know. She works with people to develop ad layouts — my dad was one of the photographers — and she mostly works in print, which means brochures and magazines. When she needs a model, she uses one of her own. She sends her models to work for other companies too, of course, but she likes the idea of being able to give her own models work.

Looking around the interior-decorated apartment, I realized how much work my mother must put into her career. I forget sometimes. When she's working at home, it doesn't seem as real as if she had to go to the office all the time.

I put the key she had given me down on the kitchen counter and opened the door to the bedroom. "Mom?"

She wasn't there. Five o'clock on a Friday afternoon, and she still wasn't there. The room looked as though a maid had just tidied it, except for the open suitcase on the bed. I sighed and backed out. The suitcase was full of my mother's clothes. This was where she was going to stay while she and my father worked out their separation. And this was where I was going to stay every second weekend, so I could spend some time with my mother.

What a joke. When did my mother ever want to spend time with me? And now she wasn't even here. I told Dad when he drove me over that I didn't want to come. He said once every two weeks wouldn't kill me, and that Mom deserved a chance to see me.

He was angry with Mom. I could tell. We both felt abandoned.

I dropped my duffle bag beside the suitcase on the bed and went back to the living room. The apartment had the silent chill of a place that had been empty all day. I found the thermostat and turned up the heat. Then I went to the refrigerator and looked for something to eat. There wasn't much, but I found a bag of English muffins and some jam. I could toast one, and the scent might make this place smell lived in, even if it was just for a while.

I was eating my second muffin and licking the jam off my fingers when I heard a key in the door, and my mother walked in.

"Kallana!" she said. She tried to smile. "How long have you been here?"

"A while."

"Well. Do you want to go out for some supper? I'll just get changed —"

"I just ate. I'm not really hungry," I said.

"Oh." Mom stepped through the foyer and took off her wool coat. She was wearing a dark pink silk suit with black pumps and a rose-and-black patterned scarf. I hadn't seen her look so elegant in a long time.

"Did you have a meeting with a client?" I asked.

"Yes. Several. I had a lunch meeting with some people from Purity Bath Products. They seemed impressed."

"I'm sure," I muttered.

"It would be a big account. Now that I've got the marketing division up and running, I can work a little more with some of the models. I've been neglecting them, lately."

"That's not all you've been neglecting," I said bitterly.

My mother paused on her way to the bedroom. "Excuse me?" she said, her voice tight.

"You heard me."

"Kallana, I don't like your tone."

"So?"

"Young lady, I have had just about enough. It's been a long day, and I don't need any hassle from you."

"No, that's right, *Mother*," I said. I felt a violent flash of anger. "You've never wanted any hassle from me, have you? You don't want to be bothered with me at all."

"That's not true," Mom said.

"Oh really? Then why did you leave?"

Mom pressed her lips together tightly, squared her shoulders and looked at me. "The issues between your father and me are the reason I left, Kallana. Not because of you."

"That's a lie. You left because you didn't want to be bothered with either of us. You left because you and your career are more important than we are." I hated the quaver in my voice. If Mom could just walk away and leave me, I certainly didn't want her to know how much I cared. I brushed away the tears that threatened to fall with a ferocious swipe of my wrist.

Mom flushed. "That's not fair, Kallana." She took a deep breath. "I've never tried to explain to you — you couldn't possibly understand ..."

Mom looked less certain. I swallowed hard. "I might."

She sat down in the chair across from me, kicking off her shoes and tossing the jacket over the armrest. She untucked her blouse and let it fall over the waistband of her skirt. I felt a little better. Watching her in her stocking feet and loosened clothes made her seem less imposing, more like a mother.

"Kall, this might be hard for you to understand. When I met your dad, I was just finishing my business degree. I was young. I knew I wanted to do something with my life. I had goals, dreams. People told me I could be anything I wanted to be, like everyone tells the young. And so I got a job. And that led to another job. And then your dad and I got married. His work as a photographer is sporadic — you know that."

I nodded. I felt some of the anger draining out of me as I listened. Mom had never talked to me like this before.

"So I kept working, but I couldn't start up the business I wanted, because it was too risky. Someone had to have a regular pay cheque to pay the bills, and it wasn't your dad. And then I had you. I worked all the time then, taking care of you, then working part-time at home while you slept. I was completely exhausted. When you finally went to school, that was my chance. And I started the modelling agency. It wasn't exactly what I wanted to do, but it was a starting place, and it was something I could do partly from home, so I was there for you after school and if you were sick.

"And the agency grew. I was proud of it. I built it, and it was growing. A year and a half ago, it seemed you'd gotten so big you didn't really need me, and I decided to start the marketing side of the business. That's what my degree trained me for, all those years ago. And I love it! Kallana, I can't help it. I love doing something where I can achieve what I want at last.

"But your dad has gotten used to me having a part-time career, and he's not adjusting well to having to help with housework and paying the bills. I've done that almost the entire time we've been married. He's not responsible with money. I want to make sure you can go on to an education. Kallana, I can't expect you to understand. But I've done the housework, paid the bills, taken care of you, cooked the meals, and worked at a job for the last twelve years. I can't do it any more. Not with the business expanding the way it is. I can't do everything. I'm not Supermom. I don't *want* to be. And if Dad isn't willing to pitch in and help me achieve my goals, then I'll have to do it on my own."

I gave a strangled sob. "Why on earth did you ever get married in the first place, then?"

Mom gave me a soft smile. "Because I loved him."

Loved. Past tense. I noticed that.

"Life is passing me by, Kall. I'm almost forty years old. It's time to start asking myself, 'What about me?'" My mother leaned back and sighed.

Yes, I thought. But what about *me*?

"But if," I said, then stopped, unable to go on. I swallowed. "But if you really loved us, nothing else would be important."

"In a perfect world, maybe." Mom tried again to smile, but the smile didn't reach her eyes. "I do love you, Kall. But in a few years you'll be grown up, and you'll have a life of your own. What do I do then?"

More to the point, I thought, feeling empty and lost inside, what do I do *now?*

Mom and I stared at each other, and the silence between us lengthened.

12

Free Throw

On Monday morning, I felt tired and droopy. The weekend with my mother had been cut short. She had to fly to Toronto on Sunday for a meeting first thing Monday with the Purity Bath people. I went home Saturday night, so she could pack and get ready to leave.

I wasn't sorry. Mom's explanation made her reasons clearer, but I still felt better with Dad. At least he seemed to care what happened to me. Even though Mom said she loved me, I still didn't think I was important to her, and that made me sad.

I wondered what my parents would do when *both* my mom and dad had to travel, or work late. What would happen to me then? Yesterday I had tried not to worry about it, and being with Dad had helped. He took me to the zoo, even though it was freezing out, and we walked around inside the buildings, watching the animals play or sleep in their dens. It was fun, and we didn't talk much. Dad seemed to know that spending Friday night and Saturday with Mom had been hard.

But now, at school, I was having trouble concentrating. I felt so hollow and sleepy, all I wanted to do was curl up in bed. By the time school was over, I wished I'd faked sick and gone home. I still didn't feel any better, and I was in no mood to face basketball practice.

Jane was getting changed when I sat down on the locker-room bench. She took one look at me and deliberately moved her sneakers from the bench beside me and put them in her locker.

I turned. "For Pete's sake, Jane. I'm not going to steal your shoes."

"I wouldn't take the chance."

I gave an exasperated sigh. "Jane, don't be an idiot."

Jane flushed.

"You guys," Marty Cassella stuck her head around the end of the row of lockers. "Cut it out. It's like ... over, okay? We're a team. We're supposed to stick together. So get over it."

Jane looked mad, but I smiled at Marty. She gave me a quick grin, then bent to lace her shoes. I quickly got into a pair of gym shorts and a clean T-shirt and hurried into the gym. Ms. Wright had already put the bins of basketballs in the centre of the court, and she was waiting for us next to them. After warming up with some stretches and ten laps around the gym, Ms. Wright beckoned us over to the bins.

"Okay, girls. Today we're going to devote practice to shooting. I want to see concentration on accuracy and technique. We'll start with standing free throws."

I felt my insides sink. Jane smirked.

"Everyone line up at the top of the key, single file. Take your shot, one person at a time, then run for the rebound. When you have your ball, take a place at the end of the line. "Understand? I want this to move quickly, girls. You all need practice at this, and this way I can watch individual technique."

I hung back as the rest of the team grabbed for the basketballs. When the bins were almost empty, I crept forward and selected a ball. Of course, the ones that were left were half-flat and squashed, but I picked the best of them and moved toward the end of the line.

The girls went through the drill quickly. Even though I had placed myself well back, my turn came faster than I'd anticipated. Chewing my lip, I glanced first at Ms. Wright, then at the girls behind me. Jane still had that smirk on her face.

"Go on, Kallana," Ms. Wright said.

"Yeah, you're holding up the line!" Jane called.

I swallowed and stared hard at the basket, lobbing the ball toward it. It curved weakly and fell with a flabby thump about ten feet away from me. The ball didn't even bounce. It was so flat, it just gave a lifeless hop and was still. I could hear the snorts of laughter behind me.

My face flaming, I bent forward to retrieve the ball and scurried to the end of the line. Even Ms. Wright was trying to suppress a smile.

"Next time, someone lend Kallana a ball, please," she called over the giggles. I tried to hunch down behind the others.

The drill began again. Everyone seemed to have their free throw technique down almost perfectly. Ms. Wright would call out things like, "Bend those knees a little more" and "Push from the legs!" And ball after ball flew through the hoop with a soft whoosh.

My insides trembled as I got closer to the front. I twitched and fidgeted. I tried not to imagine what would happen when I hit the front of the line again. Five girls were in front of me when I finally couldn't stand it any more.

"I've got to use the washroom," I muttered to Marty, who was behind me. I hurried out of the gym, my ball still gripped in my hands, and ducked into the girls' bathroom, which was just outside the gym doors.

Inside, I stopped and leaned with my back against the concrete-block wall, the chill from it penetrating my sweat-dampened T-shirt. My stomach rolled and heaved from sudden nerves, and fresh perspiration sprang out on my forehead.

What was I trying to prove out there? I couldn't keep making a fool of myself like this. I'd thought I was getting better at basketball. I was even beginning to enjoy it a little, but I couldn't keep playing if I couldn't make a free throw. It was the one part of the game where everyone in the entire gym — the players, coaches, referees, and spectators — stopped to watch. To stare. To judge.

And it was the one thing I couldn't do. I didn't understand why — it wasn't as if I hadn't tried. But it just wouldn't happen for me.

I heard the washroom door open, and before I could escape into a cubicle, Jane stepped inside.

"What are you doing in here?" she said. "Ms. Wright sent me to see why you're taking so long."

Why Jane? I asked myself silently. Why didn't she send Marty or Traci or *anyone* else?

"Tell her I'm sick," I said. "I have a stomach-ache."

"Oh, that is so lame," Jane said.

"Would you like me to barf on your shoes to prove it?"

Jane glared at me. "Why don't you just admit that you're scared? Scared like a baby to be embarrassed in front of everyone."

"I'm not scared."

"You are too. You're so used to being the queen of cool, I guess you thought you'd walk right out and be queen of the court, too. But being good at basketball takes *work*, and everyone on the team feels like a complete loser if they mess up. So grow up!"

"Listen, just shut up, okay?"

"No! I'm sick of you pretending to be a part of the team, and then running away when it looks like you won't be Queen

Kallana any more. Maybe you don't care much about this team, but I do!"

I turned to face her. "I care, all right! But you do everything you can to make me feel like an idiot out there."

"Like what?" Jane challenged.

"Just ... you know. Making me feel stupid and stuff."

"Like you've never done that to me?"

I was silent.

"Like you didn't deliberately take my shoes! Playing in that game was a big deal to me, even if it *was* only an exhibition. My parents were there!"

"For the last time, I never took your stupid shoes!" I bellowed. Jane looked startled at the sudden outburst. "Look, just leave me alone, okay?" I said fiercely. "I have enough to deal with, with my parents splitting up. I don't need to deal with crap from you, too." Then I stopped, horrified. I couldn't believe I'd just told Jane — *Jane* — about my parents' separating. But to my surprise, Jane didn't shrug it off as I had expected.

"That's too bad," she said awkwardly. "My parents almost got divorced, too, a couple of years ago. They got together again, but it was pretty rough."

"I don't want to talk about it." I said through clenched teeth. "And I don't want to hear about those dumb shoes again, okay?"

The irritation returned to Jane's face. "Why would I believe you didn't take them? I mean, it's *obvious*," she said.

"Because it really was an accident. I didn't mean to make you miss that game. I had a whole bunch of clothes and stuff on the bench, and I just scooped it up and threw it in my locker."

Jane looked at me.

"And ... I'm sorry." I muttered.

Jane regarded me steadily for a few seconds. "Okay," she said. "Let's go back to practice."

I didn't exactly want to, but I followed her out the door and back into the gym. The rest of the girls were finishing up — it was almost 4:30 and practice was over. Relieved, I went to toss my basketball into one of the bins.

"Wait," Jane said.

I stopped. "What?"

"Ms. Wright asked me to work with you on free throws."

"*Now?*"

"Yeah. So come on." Jane turned her back and walked toward the far basket. The gym had emptied out, and even Ms. Wright had disappeared — into her office, I guess. I trailed after Jane, wondering what I'd ever done to deserve this.

"Okay." Jane stood at the free throw line. "Stance has a lot to do with it. If you're stiff, it's harder to make the ball go where you want it to. So get comfortable. Bend your knees. Make sure your feet are about shoulder-width apart, so you feel balanced. Okay?"

"Okay." I tried to copy what Jane was doing, but my body felt awkward.

Jane eyed me. "You don't look right. Try putting one foot slightly forward."

I did, and that felt better.

"All right. Now hold the ball loosely, with one hand underneath. Dip your knees and push hard with your legs as you push with that one hand. Like a spring uncoiling all at once. See?" Jane demonstrated. It looked fluid and natural when she did it, but I still felt like I was made of wood when I tried.

"Again." Jane handed me the ball. "Just try popping the ball off your hand at the top of your reach. Don't aim for the basket yet."

I tried again. And again. And again. After about twenty attempts, Jane seemed satisfied.

"All right. Now try doing that and aim for the basket. Ms. Wright says to pretend you're in a phone booth, and you have to pop the ball up through the roof. The ball should arc high — you don't want it to slam against the backboard. Okay?"

My mouth felt dry. Even though there was nobody in the gym except us, actually trying to shoot still made me feel nervous. I bounced the ball a couple of times — the sound echoed in the empty space. I bent my legs and tossed the ball toward the basket, but it didn't even come close.

"No! Jane yelled. "Kallana, *think!* Do what we've just been practising!"

"I'm trying!" I flared.

"Well, try harder," Jane said. She handed me another ball from the bin.

No sympathy there, I thought. But then, that was no surprise. I exhaled and lifted the ball once more.

"Stop!" Jane commanded. "Look at what you're doing."

"What?" I gave her a blank look.

"Look at yourself. What are you doing wrong?"

I stared down at my feet. They were planted firmly together, almost ankle to ankle. My knees were straight, and I was holding the ball next to my chest.

"You have to stop and think about what your body is supposed to be doing," Jane said. "After a while, it'll be easy. You'll be able to toss free throws in your sleep, but first you have to teach your body what to do. And the only way to do that is to constantly think about it. Especially when you're scared."

I wanted to deny that last bit about me being scared, but I just kept my mouth shut and rearranged my position.

"Good! Now ready? One, two, three — spring!" Jane shouted.

I pushed hard with my legs and uncoiled my arms. I flicked my wrist at the end of the shot the way Jane had showed me. The ball sailed up, up, then arced beautifully toward the basket. It hit the rim and bounced back, but it was the closest I'd ever come to sinking a free throw.

"Way to go!" Jane whooped, grinning. "You've almost got it!" She held up her hand for me to slap her a high-five. I did, then looked at her and managed a smile.

We might not be friends, but we were making progress.

13

Playing the Game

Okay, ladies. This is it. The last two games were exhibitions, but this is the beginning of real league play. Every game counts. Every win affects our placing in the playoffs for the city championships at the end of the season. I want everyone to play their best out there. We're a team, right?"

"Yeah!" Everyone yelled.

"Okay, then." Ms. Wright put her fist out into the middle of the huddle, and Jane, Marty, and the other girls piled their hands on top. I did the same thing, but I wasn't sure what was happening until Ms. Wright and the team hollered, "1 … 2 … 3 … Go, Grizzlies!" and then flipped their fists high in the air.

I wished I still didn't feel so awkward. There was so much I didn't understand about the game, about sports in general. But what I was learning, I was beginning to like.

At the bench, Ms. Wright started giving orders. I tried to follow everything she was saying, but I still didn't understand a lot of it.

"Jane, you start centre. Kallana, you be ready to sub in switch." She noticed my panicked look. "Don't worry, I'll tell you when. Just go when I give you the signal, and play as hard as you can, okay? Rideau is a tough team."

"Right." I nodded, then settled back to watch the game. In the tip-off Jane batted the ball easily away from Rideau's centre, and Marty raced for it. She passed to Krista, one of our grade-seven players, and Jane was waiting under the basket. But a Rideau player intercepted the pass, and the game moved to our end of the court.

I found myself sitting tensely on the edge of the bench, chewing my thumbnail anxiously and watching every movement on the court.

After what seemed like hours, Ms. Wright signalled for the girls to come off. Jane was panting heavily, and the hair at Marty's temples was damp with sweat.

"Okay Kallana. Get out there. Show me what you can do."

My heart pounding, I moved off the bench and into the middle of the court. When the play resumed, I rushed toward the ball, before I remembered that when the other team had it, I was supposed to guard the centre on their team. So I backtracked and stuck to her like glue. Luckily, I was taller by at least three inches, and she had a hard time getting open to receive a pass.

"Way to cover, Kallana," Ms. Wright shouted when I knocked away a pass, and one of our players grabbed the loose ball.

I looked up and grinned, and then froze. My dad was in the stands. He was sitting quietly, but he knew I'd seen him, and he waggled his fingers at me. He hadn't told me he was coming! How was I going to play with him watching, when I was already nervous enough?

I was standing stock-still in the centre of the key. My cover had taken advantage of my confusion and chased the ball down to our end of the court, but someone from our team stole it and sent a long pass down to me. I was the only one at the opposition's end of the court.

"Get the ball, Kallie!" My dad bellowed.

My eyes snapped toward the group of players thundering down on me. The ball was sailing straight for me. I held out my hands and the ball smacked into them. I clutched it tightly, just as three members of the opposite team collided with me, and we all collapsed in a heap on the gym floor.

Phweeeet! The ref's whistle shrilled through the air. "Foul! Free throw for Meadowpark."

At first I felt relieved that we would get some advantage, but then reality sunk in. A free throw. And I was the one who had been fouled. Which meant I had to score two baskets. In front of everyone. In front of my dad!

My hands shook so badly, I could hardly grip the ball. Every game counts — I heard Ms. Wright's words echo in my head. I couldn't just walk off the court, like in practice. And I knew I wouldn't get away with pretending I was sick again.

I stood up slowly. The other players had already moved into position around the key. I moved to the very end, directly in front of the basket. It looked miles away. Had I really almost sunk a basket from here yesterday? I could never throw the ball that far and expect it to go through the rim.

"Aim for the backboard, Kallana!" Ms. Wright shouted from the sidelines.

I raised the ball to eye level, the way Jane had shown me after practice. It suddenly seemed heavy, like I had a shot-put ball in my hands instead of a basketball. My breath came in shallow gasps. Everyone was watching. If I made an idiot of myself, there was no way to hide it, no way to escape. With a quick motion, I flung the ball toward its target.

The ball fell short, not even touching the rim.

I felt myself shrink with disappointment and shame.

But my nightmare wasn't over yet. The ref caught the ball and tossed it back to me. Everyone tensed because they knew that after this shot, the ball was open. If I missed.

"Kallana!" I heard Jane's whisper from the sidelines. "Spring!"

Right. I knew what that meant. I realized my position was wrong. I got myself into the proper stance. Feet apart. Knees bent. Elbows tucked in.

I forced myself to fill my lungs with air, and then I slowly let it out. I focused my eyes on the back of the rim.

"You can do it, Kallie!" I heard my father's voice, but dimly. I clenched my jaw, and, with one fluid motion, uncoiled my body and propelled the ball with all my strength toward the hoop.

It arced through the air, just like yesterday, but this time it dropped straight through the basket. It hardly even touched the rim.

Joy and disbelief filled me like helium in a balloon. "Yes!" I cried, punching my fist in the air. I'd done it! I'd actually done it! I'd scored in a free throw. I hadn't frozen up, and I'd actually made the basket! I felt like singing and cheering and dancing all at once. I'd never felt so fantastic in my entire life!

14

Me and My Dad

Ms. Wright put Jane back in, and I came thankfully off the court. The whole team was fired up after I scored that last basket. I'd never gotten so many back slaps and compliments for something I'd done before.

I watched the action on the court. As the clock wound down, things got more intense. Rideau fought hard to hold their two-point lead. I chewed my thumbnail as Jane swiped the ball from her opponent and thundered to centre court. Twelve seconds were left on the clock.

Jane stopped, pivoted away from a Rideau player, and fired the ball from where she stood. It sailed through the air and plunked neatly through the basket for a three-pointer. The buzzer blasted. Meadowpark won — 56–55.

Our whole team went wild. The first game of the season — and we'd won it! Everyone jumped up and down in a knot of bodies, our arms entwined, screaming until our throats were hoarse. I'd never felt anything like it. I'd never been a part of something like that before. Inside, I bubbled and sparkled like champagne trapped in a bottle, and I laughed when Jane dumped the water bucket over all of us. My hair was dripping, I was sweaty, and my uniform was still hideous. I knew I'd never looked less beautiful, but I didn't care. At that moment, it didn't matter. Ms. Wright went around congratulating us and saying things like, "Great game, girls" and "That's the kind of effort I like to see!"

After we finished celebrating and shook hands with the other team, I climbed up the bleachers to my dad.

"Hey, kiddo." He pulled on a straggly lock of my hair. "So you're going to be the female equivalent of Michael Jordan, are you?"

"Well, maybe not yet," I laughed. "I think I'd better play a few more games first."

"I was proud of you, Kallie. You were terrific." Dad smiled at me.

Pride seemed to swell in my throat, and I couldn't speak. Dad reached over and tousled my hair. "I wish Mom could have seen you play," he said.

I sat down beside him and looked out at the gym. "Even if she wasn't away, she wouldn't have wanted to," I said.

Dad was silent a moment. "I think she would have. I don't want you to think she doesn't care about you, Kallie. I know she does. She just has a lot of her own issues to deal with right now."

"Yeah, I know," I said bitterly. "We talked about some of them last Friday."

"What did she say?"

"Just that she's tired of not being able to do what she wants — that she wants her big, exciting career, and pretty soon I'll be grown up and won't need her any more, anyway."

Dad rubbed the stubble on his chin with one hand. "Well, that's some of it. Your Mom has always been very ambitious. It was hard for her to put aside her goals to take care of a family after we got married and had you. And I guess my career hasn't helped much, in that respect. But making a lot of money was never as important to me as spending time with you and Mom and doing what I really like to do. And photography is what I really like to do."

"Why doesn't Mom feel that way?"

"She does. But what she wants is to feel important and to achieve. To get somewhere, fast. I've never completely understood where. But money is a kind of milestone for a lot of people, Mom included. If you have a certain amount, you're successful. If you have a certain amount more, then you're more successful. It's like a measuring stick."

"So spending time with us isn't important to her?"

"Oh, I think it is. She wouldn't have nudged her career aside even for a second when you were born if it wasn't. But she did. I think she's frustrated right now — has been frustrated for years — and she's got tunnel vision about her career at the moment. Nothing else seems as important right now."

"But Mom's been working for years. It's not like she's been a housewife and suddenly decided she wants to go back to work."

"I know. But Mom has been trying to be a homemaker and create a successful business, and that's pretty tough, I guess."

I paused. "Do you still love her?" My heart gave a quick thump, waiting for his answer.

Dad gave a half smile. "Yes. I do. In spite of everything, in spite of the problems, I still love her. I don't think I've been exactly easy to get along with, and I've been pretty angry with her. But I do still love her."

That was comforting. Thank goodness my dad was so honest with me. It was something I had always loved about him — he never treated me like he thought I was a baby who wouldn't understand. But the question I really needed answered, I still hadn't asked.

"Do you think you and Mom will get back together?"

Dad sighed. "I don't know, Kallie. I hope so, but your mom has to decide what she wants. I can't make that decision for her. There are other things we need to work out. Her career isn't the only one."

I slumped on the bench. I wanted to hate my mother, but I couldn't. I wanted her to be happy. I wanted us to be happy. Why couldn't we all be happy together? Why did people have to want different things?

Maybe Mom did want to be with us, deep down inside. Maybe she just needed time to figure things out. I guess all I could do was hope. But for now, at least I had my dad. And even though I knew he wasn't perfect, I also knew he loved me. I was suddenly very glad that he'd come to the game. He'd seen me score a free throw — something I hadn't been sure I'd ever be able to do.

Dad hugged me with one arm. "Want to go out to The Golden Dragon for supper to celebrate winning the game?"

I was about to say okay, when Jane came back in the gym.

"Kallana? We've been looking all over for you. The whole team and Ms. Wright are going out for pizza. Want to come?"

I looked at my dad. "Is it okay?"

"Of course. After all, you're part of a team now, right?"

I squeezed my father's hand. "Oh, I don't know. Maybe I always was. A family is kind of a team, isn't it?"

"Sure is. And a family can be big, or it can be just the two of us."

I smiled a real smile at Jane. "Can my dad come with me?"

"Yeah. Most of the parents are coming. Come and get changed. We're meeting there in fifteen minutes." Jane disappeared through the gym doors, and as I clambered down the bleachers, I was glad. Glad to be Kallana, and that was a new feeling. Just Kallana — not Kallana the fashion queen, not Kallana the clique master, not Kallana, queen of the court. Just Kallana.

And it felt *great!*

Other books you'll enjoy in the Sports Stories series ...

Baseball

☐ *Curve Ball* by John Danakas #1
Tom Poulos is looking forward to a summer of baseball in Toronto until his mother puts him on a plane to Winnipeg.

☐ *Baseball Crazy* by Martyn Godfrey #10
Rob Carter wins an all-expenses-paid chance to be batboy at the Blue Jays spring training camp in Florida.

☐ *Shark Attack* by Judi Peers #25
The East City Sharks have a good chance of winning the county championship until their arch rivals get a tough new pitcher.

☐ *Hit and Run* by Dawn Hunter and Karen Hunter #35
Glen Thomson is a talented pitcher, but as his ego inflates, team morale plummets. Will he learn from being benched for losing his temper?

Basketball

☐ *Fast Break* by Michael Coldwell #8
Moving from Toronto to small-town Nova Scotia was rough, but when Jeff makes the school basketball team he thinks things are looking up.

☐ *Camp All-Star* by Michael Coldwell #12
In this insider's view of a basketball camp, Jeff Lang encounters some unexpected challenges.

☐ *Nothing but Net* by Michael Coldwell #18
The Cape Breton Grizzly Bears prepare for an out-of-town basketball tournament they're sure to lose.

☐ *Slam Dunk* by Steven Barwin and Gabriel David Tick #23
In this sequel to *Roller Hockey Blues*, Mason Ashbury's basketball team adjusts to the arrival of some new players: girls.

☐ *Hockey Night in Transcona* by John Danakas #7
Cody Powell gets promoted to the Transcona Sharks first line, bumping out the coach's son who's not happy with the change.

☐ *Face Off* by C.A. Forsyth #13
A talented hockey player finds himself competing with his best friend for a spot on a select team.

☐ *Hat Trick* by Jacqueline Guest #20
The only girl on an all-boys' hockey team works to earn the captain's respect and her mother's approval.

☐ *Hockey Heroes* by John Danakas #22
A left-winger on the thirteen-year-old Transcona Sharks adjusts to a new best friend and his mom's boyfriend.

☐ *Hockey Heat Wave* by C.A. Forsyth #27
In this sequel to *Face Off*, Zack and Mitch encounter some trouble when it looks like only one of them will make the select team at hockey camp.

☐ *Shoot to Score* by Sandra Richmond #31
Playing defence on the B list alongside the coach's mean-spirited son is a tough obstacle for Steven to overcome, but he perseveres and changes his luck.

Riding

☐ *A Way With Horses* by Peter McPhee #11
A young Alberta rider invited to study show jumping at a posh local riding school uncovers a secret.

☐ *Riding Scared* by Marion Crook #15
A reluctant new rider struggles to overcome her fear of horses.

☐ *Katie's Midnight Ride* by C.A. Forsyth #16
An ambitious barrel racer finds herself without a horse weeks before her biggest rodeo.

☐ *Glory Ride* by Tamara L. Williams #21
Chloe Anderson fights memories of a tragic fall for a place on the Ontario Young Riders' Team.

☐ *Cutting it Close* by Marion Crook #24
In this novel about barrel racing, a talented young rider finds her horse is in trouble just as she is about to compete in an important event.

☐ *Shadow Ride* by Tamara L. Williams #37
Bronwen has to choose between competing aggressively for herself or helping out a teammate.

Roller Hockey

☐ *Roller Hockey Blues* by Steven Barwin and Gabriel David Tick #17
Mason Ashbury faces a summer of boredom until he makes the roller-hockey team.

Running

☐ *Fast Finish* by Bill Swan #30
Noah is a promising young runner headed for the provincial finals when he suddenly decides to withdraw from the event.

Sailing

☐ *Sink or Swim* by William Pasnak #5
Dario can barely manage the dog paddle, but thanks to his mother he's spending the summer at a water sports camp.

Soccer

☐ *Lizzie's Soccer Showdown* by John Danakas #3
When Lizzie asks why the boys and girls can't play together, she finds herself the new captain of the soccer team.

☐ *Alecia's Challenge* by Sandra Diersch #32
Thirteen-year-old Alecia has to cope with a new school, a new stepfather and friends who have suddenly discovered the opposite sex.

☐ *Shut-Out!* by Camilla Reghelini Rivers #39
David wants to play soccer more than anything, but will the new coach let him?

Swimming

☐ *Water Fight!* by Michele Martin Bossley #14
Josie's perfect sister is driving her crazy but when she takes up swimming — Josie's sport — it's too much to take.

☐ *Taking a Dive* by Michele Martin Bossley #19
Josie holds the provincial record for the butterfly, but in this sequel to *Water Fight,* she can't seem to match her own time and might not go on to the nationals.

☐ *Great Lengths* by Sandra Diersch #26
Fourteen-year-old Jessie decides to find out whether the rumours about a new swimmer at her Vancouver club are true.

Track and Field

☐ *Mikayla's Victory* by Cynthia Bates #29
Mikayla must compete against her friend if she wants to represent her school at an important track event.